SO-AXK-790

How would she ever keep her wits about her around this family?

"If you'll excuse me, Mrs. Farrington, I would like to go to my room now. The meal was delicious." Deborah pushed back her chair then hesitated. "I'd like to get my patterns and fabric organized. Which room did you want me to use for sewing?"

"The one adjoining your bedroom," Adell replied. "Margarita will show you."

"Surely you don't plan to start working the first evening you're here?" Ridge said, rising to his feet. "Perhaps later we could all have iced tea out on the veranda."

Deborah saw Adell's frown, and responded quickly. "No, thank you," she murmured. "I have work to do. Good evening." She hurried out of the dining room and down the hall, but was still in earshot of Adell's response to her son.

"Don't be trying to impress her, dear. You have enough lady friends. Let's not add the hired help to your list."

Deborah gasped, clutching the banister to refrain herself from tearing back into the room and giving Adell a sample of her temper. Ridge's muted response held a sharp note of impatience, but this scarcely salved her wound. She turned and flew up the steps, venting her rage in a flash of speed. She burst into her room and slammed the door, her cheeks flaming.

How could she possibly stay here an entire summer? How? She clenched her fists in the folds of her skirt.

CIMARRON SUNSET

Peggy Darty

Serenade/Saga
BOOKS
of the Zondervan Publishing House
Grand Rapids, Michigan

A Note From The Author:
I love to hear from my readers! You may correspond with me by writing:

> Peggy Darty
> 1415 Lake Drive, S.E.
> Grand Rapids, MI 49506

CIMARRON SUNSET
Copyright © 1985 by Peggy Darty
Grand Rapids, Michigan

Serenade/Serenata is an imprint of Zondervan Publishing House,
1415 Lake Drive, S.E., Grand Rapids, Michigan 49506.

ISBN 0-310-47262-8

All rights reserved. No part of this publication may be reproduced, stored in a retrieval system, or transmitted in any form or by any means—electronic, mechanical, photocopy, recording, or any other—except for brief quotations in printed reviews, without the prior permission of the publisher.

Printed in the United States of America

86 87 88 89 90 91 / 10 9 8 7 6 5 4 3 2

For Lan, Steve, and Darla

CHAPTER 1

Los Angeles
August 1, 1884

DEBORAH HOLT STARED GLUMLY through the carriage window to the passing shops along Spring Street. Soon the town would give way to barren countryside, dry and dusty, and whatever awaited her could not possibly be as pleasant as the cozy rooms she and her mother shared in town. So far there was nothing comforting about her trip at all; certainly not her relationship with the woman seated across from her. From the corner of her eye she saw the woman's sullen expression falling on her. Deborah shifted nervously, rustling the taffeta of her flowing emerald skirt.

Her eyes, the color of the dress her mother had made to match them, clouded momentarily as she tried to imagine what the future held for her at this woman's ranch. What was it called—Cimarron?

Her thoughts were interrupted by Mrs. Farrington's now familiar voice. "I imagine you dislike me, young lady."

Ever so slowly, Deborah turned to face her. "No, I don't dislike you."

Adell responded by snapping open her black lace fan, and fluttering it beneath her double chin. Deborah thought that Mrs. Farrington might be considered attractive, in her gray silk gown and elaborate, silver curls if there had been any kindness in her flushed round face. But the blue eyes that swept Deborah were as cold as winter ice on the Santa Monicas.

"Well, it's a pity your mother had to be so careless with my most expensive gown and cloak."

The small features in Deborah's face tensed momentarily as she carefully chose her words. "Mother isn't normally careless," she said. "She has the reputation of being the most skilled seamstress in Los Angeles. She wasn't feeling her best this morning."

"That's no excuse for knocking an inkwell onto a customer's best dress! Do you have any idea what a Paris gown costs? No, of course you don't." She dismissed the discussion with a wave of her hand and turned to glare out the window.

Deborah, too, sought refuge in the distant orange groves on the edge of town. Still, the white silk gown, blotched with ink stains, sprang unbidden into her mind. She sighed, leaning her head against the cushioned seat. Her mother had asked her to accept the arrangement, knowing how hopeless it was to deter Adell Farrington from getting her way. They could not afford to buy her a new gown, and they could think of no other solution.

"Well," Adell tapped the fan against her gloved

hand, "perhaps your services for the summer will make amends; and it will be a relief to have a seamstress in residence at Cimarron, despite your inexperience."

"I am nineteen years old, Mrs. Farrington. I assure you my work is as good as anyone's!" Deborah's temper began to flare, despite her resolve to keep calm.

"Humph." The thin brows arched thoughtfully. "Well, let's hope so. Victoria and I both need adjustments to our garments. And we have friends arriving from Santa Fe later in the month. No doubt, they'll need a few seams repaired after a jolting ride out on the Southern Pacific."

Deborah turned inquisitive eyes to the woman whose husband was a major stockholder in the Southern Pacific Railroad Company. It seemed strange to hear her speak of the railroad with such disdain. She turned back to the distant foothills, recalling her own bitterness toward the railroad after her father's tragic death. They had hoped the railroad job, and subsequent move west, would be the answer to his dream. Instead it had contributed to his early death. Still, with God's help, she and her mother had survived.

Yet, how could she survive three months at this woman's ranch? How could she bite her tongue and be polite when she had never before refrained from absolute honesty? And most of all, how could she be civil to a woman who had treated her mother so cruelly?

"In everything give thanks for this is the will of God." Her father's voice echoed through her mind, quoting the verse he so often applied to their trying situations. She and her parents had always shaped their lives by the Scriptures, and though her father was no longer with them, the legacy of his teaching had kept them strong.

"We're on Cimarron land now," Adell swept a gloved hand through the window.

Deborah studied the landscape curiously.

The flatness of Los Angeles lay behind them now. Here, surprisingly, was a rich, green valley cupped by chaparral foothills and bordered by a distant stream.

Barbed wire enclosed grazing cattle—more cattle than Deborah had ever seen in her life! Just ahead, a knot of men were grouped beside a campfire where several red-and-white calves sprawled, their legs bound with rope.

"What are they doing?" Deborah asked, glancing back at Mrs. Farrington.

Adell leaned over to look out the window. The perfume, like the woman, was overpowering. "They're branding," she said simply.

The carriage slowed and stopped as the driver called a greeting to the ranch hands. Sun-bronzed faces turned, men waved. Then suddenly, the weary faces were lit by an expression of pleasure as they spotted the young woman within. All made a swipe for their wide felt hats—all except the man whose head was bent over the hot iron and the struggling calf. Deborah smiled briefly at the nods in her direction, but her attention was drawn by the man intent on his work.

He seemed taller, more muscular, than the others. Probably a foreman, Deborah decided. He tilted his head to glance at the carriage, and under his dusty hat she saw a mass of dark curls. The hot sun filtered over rigid cheekbones, aquiline nose, squared jaw and chin. The eyes met hers—eyes the color of the dark smoke rising from the fire. The wide, careless smile on his face suggested he was not bothered by the blazing sun, or the branding iron in his hand, or the protesting calf.

She intended to look away from his gaze, but nevertheless waited a moment longer than she knew was proper. With a polite nod, he turned back to his task, applying the hot iron to the calf's hip. The sickening singe brought a sympathetic gasp to Deborah's throat.

"That seems so cruel," she cried, glancing at Adell.

"Cruel but necessary, I'm afraid," Adell said. "Otherwise, how could we identify our cattle? And what's to keep some thief from stealing us blind?"

Considering her words, Deborah turned to look again at the poor calf, and the strange man bent over him. "Perhaps," she conceded. "But it must take a calloused individual to do the branding."

Her eyes lingered on the tall, broad-shouldered man as he stood, absently brushing the dust from his leather chaps. Like the others, he wore the jeans that Mr. Strauss of San Francisco had made so popular, with vest and loose shirt. Unlike the others, there was an air about him that made him different, something Deborah sensed but could not define.

"Calloused?" Adell echoed, as the carriage rocked into motion again. "No, he isn't a calloused man, just a very determined one. He does whatever he wishes and the others do not challenge him. He's my son."

Deborah's mouth dropped open. Before she could stop herself, she whirled around for a second look. The carriage had moved on, however, and the sea of cattle was replaced by a pasture of sleek horses, whose coats gleamed like satin in the bright sunlight. *Adell Farrington's son a ranch hand?* Deborah silently questioned, staring blankly at the horses.

She pressed her lips together to seal any careless words. She felt Adell's eyes probing her again, but she dared not ask any more questions. Still, the memory of the sun-bronzed cowboy lingered in her mind.

The dirt road snaked through the heart of the valley. To the north, opposite the horse corrals, a cluster of small adobe bunkhouses dotted the landscape. A roofed breezeway connected the buildings where saddles, ropes, and bridles hung.

Deborah watched as the road fanned out, paralleling the grassland filled with leafy oaks and rosebushes. Through the branches of the oaks, Deborah caught a flash of red that she soon identified as a tile roof; another turn and the sprawling, adobe hacienda came into view. Wide verandas swept the front and sides of the whitewashed structure where huge enameled pots of geraniums and bougainvillaea added a cheerful welcome. As the carriage ground to a stop, the driver yelled a greeting to a young Spaniard, dressed in a loose white shirt and dark trousers. The smile on his face seemed frozen as he opened the door and helped first Adell then Deborah down.

A small, blonde girl in a white, ruffled dress stood on the veranda. A limp braid hung to her tiny waist, while a thin fringe of light bangs brushed her forehead and framed her pale face. A familiar sharpness stamped on the girl's features identified her to Deborah as Mrs. Farrington's daughter, yet the round blue eyes were soft and deep, unlike the cold, protruding eyes of her mother.

"Hello, dear," Adell placed her large hand on the girl's narrow shoulder.

Deborah caught the faint, almost imperceptible shrug of the girl's shoulder before Adell withdrew her hand.

"This is my daughter, Victoria," Adell glanced back at Deborah. "Victoria, this is Miss Deborah Holt. She will be staying with us for a while."

"Why?" the girl demanded suspiciously.

"She's going to do some sewing for us," Adell replied crisply. "Now where's Margarita? I need my tea. I've had a horrendous morning! Roberto, take Miss Holt's trunk to the bedroom at the end of the upper hall, the gold one. If you'll excuse me, I must rest now."

"Come on." Victoria huffed a bored sigh, one that Deborah suspected was feigned. She sensed that the girl was far too curious about her presence at Cimarron to be bored. "I'll take you to your room," the girl called, twirling her tiny frame around to lead the way. As she pushed the door wide, she could not resist turning to ask, "Just why *did* you come?"

"To sew for you, as your mother said. And I understand you'll be having guests this month."

The girl's thin lips rounded in a pout. "The Warrens from Santa Fe."

Within the house, Deborah caught only a brief glimpse of marble tile, ornate chandeliers, and mahogany furnishings as she hurried after Victoria up the circular stairway. At the top of the stairs, the dimness cleared, offset by sconces of lit candles along the white plastered walls. Red Brussels carpet ran the length of the hall, past several closed doors, all handsomely carved in dark wood. At the end of the long hall,

Victoria threw open a door and dashed inside the room.

Deborah caught up, then hesitated in the arched doorway. The walls were papered in gold brocade, a gold that was repeated in velvet drapes and spread. Lace curtains fluttered before a narrow window that stretched from ceiling to floor.

"This is lovely," Deborah smiled, her glance trailing over the cherry commode, wardrobe, and four-poster bed. Once her eyes found the comfortable-looking bed, every bone in her body made a silent plea for rest.

Roberto shuffled up behind her, and she quickly stepped aside so that he could heave the trunk onto the floor at the foot of the bed.

"Gracias," she smiled at him.

He bowed low then dashed from the room.

Deborah glanced back at Victoria, who was leaning against a bedpost, eyeing her curiously.

"Where's your bedroom?" Deborah asked to break the silence.

"The first one on the left at the top of the stairs. Mother and Father have the next two adjoining rooms. Ridge lives with the ranch hands."

"Ridge?"

"Ridge is my brother," the girl continued in her bored tone. "He'd rather associate with the workers than with us. He does have a bunkhouse to himself, though," she added, begrudgingly elevating his status.

"I see," Deborah removed her leghorn hat and brushed at the trailing strands of her dark hair. "I hope we can be friends, Victoria."

"Call me Torie. I hate the name Victoria. Only Mother calls me that. My brother's name is Breckenridge. He prefers Ridge."

14

"All right, I'll call you Torie." Deborah said with a smile.

"I imagine Margarita will be bringing up fresh water for you if you want to wash up. Are you going to start sewing now?"

"Oh, not now!" Deborah laughed. "First, I'm going to rest."

"Grown-ups always have to *rest*," Torie heaved a disgusted sigh and flounced out of the room with a loud slam of the door.

Deborah stared after her for a moment, wondering how she could befriend the spoiled girl.

Her worries were soon forgotten, however, as she dropped onto the feather mattress that seemed to envelop her small body instantly. She snuggled deeper, her dark lashes drooping. A lace curtain fluttered against the open window as the oak leaves rustled, bringing a fresh breeze into the room. Deborah gave an exhausted sigh and drifted off to sleep.

A vague though steady knock tugged at Deborah's consciousness. She tried to ignore the offensive sound, but it persisted. Finally, her sleepy eyes opened and circled the room. She became aware of a muted voice calling to her beyond the closed door.

"Who is it?" she asked, her eyes widening as the door slowly opened, and a plump, middle-aged Spanish woman entered balancing a china pitcher of water. "Señorita, you want water for bathing?" she asked, a tentative smile on her lips.

"Yes, thank you."

The woman was dressed in colorful calico and her dark hair was wound into shiny braids on the top of her head. She hurried across the room, placing the

15

water on a marble-topped table. Then she laid out soap and a cloth.

"Thank you," Deborah smiled. "Gracias."

"I am Margarita," she said, dark eyes shining.

"Hello, Margarita. I'm Deborah Holt." She was delighted to return Margarita's glowing smile, grateful for the genuine friendliness she felt in her, particularly after spending time with Adell and her daughter.

"Soon we will be dining," Margarita said, looking at Deborah's rumpled clothing.

"Oh!" Deborah swung off the bed. "Then I must hurry."

"Si," the woman nodded agreeably then left the room.

Deborah pulled her fingers through her mass of hair, wondering how quickly she could make herself presentable, when the sound of male voices drifted up to her from the open window. Curiously, she walked over to peer out. Rosebushes, palms, and oaks filled the yard. Directly below her, Roberto stood beside a sequoia post on the veranda, apparently conversing with someone just under the eaves. Deborah strained to see who, but the adobe wall blocked her view.

"Señor, they're coming in by night," Roberto was saying. "When I was returning from town last evening, I heard horses nickering at the upper end of the canyon."

"Thank you for telling me, Roberto," a deep male voice replied. "I'll put a guard up there tonight. We can't afford to keep losing our cattle. And now, you've earned your mustang."

"Señor! Gracias!" Roberto clapped his hands with joy.

Deborah tried to force herself back from the

window, suddenly aware that she was eavesdropping. Just before she turned to leave, however, a tall, broad-shouldered man stepped into her line of vision. He lifted a pair of broad, tanned hands to grasp Roberto's narrow shoulders.

"The mustang is yours," he repeated.

"Gracias!" Roberto whooped. "Gracias, Señor Farrington!"

At the sound of that name, Deborah shot back from the window, her mind filled with the memory of the man bent over the calf. She stared blankly at the fluttering lace curtain, fighting back an insane desire to peer out again. Yet, how foolish she would feel if those dark gray eyes drifted up to the second story window and caught her staring and eavesdropping.

She squared her shoulders and marched resolutely to the pitcher of water. But the deep male laughter seemed to trail her, a full rich sound from a man who obviously enjoyed life.

This man is Adell Farrington's son, she thought, bewildered. It seemed impossible.

CHAPTER 2

DEBORAH SNEAKED A GLANCE down the lace-covered dining table to Stuart Farrington, the head of the household. He was thin, of medium build, with dark hair and skin. His quiet distinction was enhanced by the dark suit and black cravat knotted at his throat. Suddenly the pale brown eyes lifted from his crystal water goblet and shot directly to her.

She shifted uncomfortably, quickly spearing her silver fork into the enchilada on her plate. He was an observant, perceptive man, despite his coolly detached countenance. He had only looked at her twice since their introduction, but in those brief calculating glances, he seemed to look right through her, perceiving her innermost thoughts.

Adell sat at the opposite end of the table, stiffly aloof, still complaining of her headache. Torie sat to Deborah's right, picking over the sumptuous feast that Margarita had prepared.

Deborah darted a glance at the empty chair opposite

her, relieved that the mysterious son was not present. The tension overhanging the room was enough to make her forget her table manners; she didn't need any more distractions.

Only the clatter of silver on the plate and the occasional clink of ice in a goblet broke the silence. Deborah swallowed, absently smoothing a wrinkle from her starched, white shirtwaist.

Suddenly, a door banged and heavy footsteps resounded on the marble hall.

Adell looked up expectantly, a soft light warming the depths of her blue eyes.

"Dear, you're late," she said, her tone mildly reproving.

The footsteps approached the dining room, then halted somewhere behind Deborah's chair. The skin on the back of her neck prickled; she sensed eyes boring into her.

"I was down at the bunkhouse having a little fun with the boys," the deep voice returned, his tone pleasant.

"Really, dear," Adell gave a short laugh, "you shouldn't be so friendly with the hired help. They're apt to take advantage of you."

A laugh rumbled from the direction of the footsteps. "I doubt it," he said, stopping beside Deborah's chair.

Deborah swallowed her food and glanced cautiously at the staring stranger. He was dressed casually in a loose-fitting shirt, dungarees, and brown leather vest. His hair was neatly combed, yet long enough to brush the collar of his shirt. When their eyes met she was certain she was going to choke. The eyes—soft, hazy, and dark—again had a strange effect on her.

Adell cleared her throat. "Breckenridge, this is Miss Deborah Holt. She's come out to do some work for me. Miss Holt, my son Breckenridge Farrington."

"How do you do," Deborah murmured.

"Good evening." White teeth flashed against sunbronzed skin. "It's a pleasure to have you at Cimarron, Miss Holt." He settled his long frame into the chair opposite her, then lifted a snowy linen napkin and spread it over his lap. "What kind of work will you be doing here?" he asked.

Deborah's lips parted to voice a response but Adell was quicker.

"She will be sewing for me," she replied crisply. "Are you very hungry, dear?"

"Ravenous." He grinned at Deborah. "Sewing is essential work here since Margarita's cooking has caused us all to overindulge."

"Not *me*," Torie said.

"Did they finish the branding?" Stuart Farrington finally spoke. His tone, like Adell's, had warmed as he addressed his son, whom Deborah now saw as a taller, broader version of himself.

"We're almost finished. Incidentally, I have given Roberto the mustang."

"Roberto hardly has time to ride," Adell interrupted.

"Then allow him time, Mother! Surely you know an employee will be happier and thus work harder, if you treat him well. Don't you agree, Miss Holt?"

Deborah glanced up in surprise. Despite the color rising to her cheeks, she kept her voice even. "Yes, I suppose so," she answered.

Torie, who had been watching silently, thrust her plate back and fixed her pale blue eyes on Deborah. "What are you going to sew for *me?*"

20

Deborah smiled at her. "Whatever you need."

The girl whirled in her chair toward her mother. "I want one of those new tennis dresses, Mother. Everyone is talking about tennis."

"Dear, you know you cannot play—"

"I want to learn." Her small chin jutted out defiantly.

"When you're stronger," her mother said, with a glance down the table toward her husband.

"I'll never be strong!" Torie blurted out. "You won't let me be. I thought that was one reason we moved out here. A better climate, you said. And there'd be sunshine and warm weather most of the year. So far, all I do is sit on the porch and *look* at the sunshine. I hate it here. I'm bored to death!"

With that she flung her napkin down and dashed from the table.

Deborah averted her shocked eyes to her plate. She had never seen a child act so, at least not without a reprimand.

Stuart Farrington cleared his throat. "Well, Victoria seems out of sorts tonight."

"Torie seems to be out of sorts most of the time," Ridge said. "Maybe Miss Holt can liven her up a bit. Have you learned this new sport, Miss Holt?"

"No, I haven't," she replied, her eyes moving cautiously from his blazing smile to Adell's scowl.

"Then maybe we can learn together—you, Torie, and I. Mother, we need to prepare an area here for playing tennis. It will be good exercise for Torie."

"We shall see," Adell replied stiffly.

Margarita swept into the dining room, bearing a platter of steaming banana fritters. Deborah looked doubtfully at the desert, wondering how they could

21

possibly eat more. She understood the family's sudden weight gain, and realized she would do so likewise if she allowed herself to overindulge.

"If you'll excuse me, Mrs. Farrington, I would like to go to my room now. The meal was delicious." Deborah pushed back her chair then hesitated. "I'd like to get my patterns and fabric organized. Which room did you want me to use for sewing?"

"The one adjoining your bedroom," Adell replied. "Margarita will show you."

"Surely you don't plan to start working the first evening you're here?" Breckenridge said, rising to his feet. "Perhaps later we could all have iced tea out on the veranda."

Deborah saw Adell's frown, and responded quickly. "No, thank you," she murmured. "I have work to do. Good evening." She hurried out of the dining room and down the hall, but was still in earshot of Adell's response to her son.

"Don't be trying to impress her, Breckenridge. You have enough lady friends. Let's not add the hired help to your list."

Deborah gasped, clutching the banister to refrain herself from tearing back into the room and giving Adell a sample of her temper. Ridge's muted response held a sharp note of impatience, but this scarcely salved her wound. She turned and flew up the steps, venting her rage in a flash of speed. She burst into her room and slammed the door, her cheeks flaming.

How could she possibly stay here an entire summer? How? She clenched her fists in the folds of her skirt.

Slow steps were shuffling down the hall, followed by a soft knock on her door. Deborah whirled, ready to do battle as she yanked the door open to find Margarita standing there.

The sight of the woman's compassionate face brought a heavy sigh to Deborah's tight chest as she silently motioned her in.

"Señorita, it will be all right." Margarita's plump hand touched her arm.

Deborah stared at her, wishing with all of her heart that she could believe that. It would take patience and prayer and a tight reign on her temper!

"I appreciate your kindness, Margarita," she responded, her anger slowly melting under the woman's sympathetic smile.

"Graçias," Margarita called over her shoulder, lighting the lamps then opening the door to an adjoining room.

Deborah peered in as Margarita carried the lamp inside. The room was small, containing only a single bed, a chest and a desk, but it would be perfect for her sewing room.

"This will be fine," she offered Margarita an appreciative smile. "Thank you."

Margarita nodded and patted her arm again, then turned and hurried from the room.

Deborah stared after her, deciding that the safest method of dealing with Adell would be to avoid her. Perhaps she would consider taking some of her meals in her room. Or better yet, she would join Margarita in the kitchen. After all, she was only the hired help!

Yes, she would simply ignore Adell, she decided smugly. Or would she? What had her father once told her? Love your enemies, do good to those who despised you. Could she do that? There *was* such a thing as righteous anger, she reminded herself. She couldn't just stand still and suffer abuse.

In an effort to divert her thoughts, she leaned down and opened her trunk, deciding to complete her unpacking. Before long, the door slipped open and Torie thrust her head around the corner.

"What are you doing?" the girl asked, her face set in its perpetual expression of boredom.

"Just unpacking," Deborah replied, shaking out a blue sateen dress.

"You have pretty clothes." Torie sauntered over to entwine an arm around the bedpost. "Did you make that dress?"

"I make all my clothes. I've been sewing since I was very young."

"My age?" Torie asked, tilting her head.

"How old are you?"

"Fourteen."

"At fourteen I was learning different stitches." Deborah's eyes turned wistful. "My father had a mercantile store back in Kansas, and Mother kept a small room in the back for sewing dresses from the bolts of material we stocked."

"I can't do *anything*!" Torie cried, her small mouth drawn into a sullen pout.

"Oh, I'll bet you can." Deborah hung up the dress and sat down on the side of the bed near her. "I'll bet you can do lots of things if you put your mind to it."

"They won't let me!" she wailed.

Deborah bit her lip, wondering how to respond. Apparently the child had been ill, and her parents had doubtlessly shielded her to the point of being overprotective.

"Well, maybe I'll teach you to sew on buttons," she suggested on an impulse.

"That sounds dull," Torie frowned. "What's so special about sewing on buttons?"

"Matching up colors. That can be fun. Perhaps you could think of it as some kind of an art project."

"Art? I like art." She twirled her long braid around her tiny fingers. "I was taking classes in oil painting before we moved out here." Her pleasant expression faded. "I don't know why we had to come all the way to California. Father bought stock in the railroad like other men, but not all of the others moved."

"Well, some men just seem to feel the call of the West," Deborah sighed. "My father did."

"What did your father come here to do?" Torie asked.

Deborah hesitated, her thoughts slipping back to the tall slim man who had given her so much love and tenderness. "He joined the railroad. He had never done manual labor before, but he had a dream of coming to California. He thought working on the railroad would provide him that opportunity, and an income for us once we arrived."

"Does he still work for the railroad?" Torie yawned.

Deborah was silent for a moment, staring at her battered old trunk. "No. He was helping lay rails across a ravine. He . . . there was an accident. He was killed."

"Oh." Torie stared at her for a moment. "What did you do then?"

"We didn't have the money to return home, so Mother and I stayed in Los Angeles."

Torie nodded, her eyes dropping curiously to the contents of Deborah's trunk. "What's that book?" she asked.

"It's a fashion book," Deborah responded, reconciled to the fact that she would not be unpacking in

25

private. But the little girl was lonely and needed a friend, she reminded herself as she lifted the book to the bed and opened its dusty pages. "My mother and I use it as a guide in designing dresses. See. Here's a Renoir print of a dress that ladies back East and in Europe are wearing."

The dress was of magenta silk, trimmed with feathers and lace, featuring a long draped skirt.

Torie leaned over the book, one slim hand absently brushing at her bangs. "How do you make those awful looking bustles?" she complained, studying the back view of the dress.

"We sew a straw cushion into the skirt, and put steel loops in the lining to maintain the shape. Then we make a crinolette to go underneath. It's very complicated."

"I hate my mother's bustles. They make her look like a duck. Back in Santa Fe, my brother used to bring pretty girls to the ranch. They wore dresses that were soft and lacy *without* the bustles. But that was years ago when he lived with us. . . ." her voice, like her thoughts, trailed off.

Deborah scooped up the book and turned back to the trunk. She could imagine that the dark and charming Ridge would have brought many girls to their ranch. But it was of no concern to her.

"This is the first time he's lived with us in a long time," Torie continued, looking at Deborah.

Deborah busied herself with her unpacking, determined not to show any interest in the bachelor brother. She added the fashion book to the stack of fabric on the bed and took the load to the adjoining room. Torie tagged along after her.

"Are you going to make a sewing room in here?" she asked, lingering in the door.

"Yes. It will be perfect," Deborah glanced appreciatively around the room. "And it's almost as big as my corner of the sewing shop Mother and I have in Los Angeles."

Torie's little nose quirked distastefully. "I think it would be dull to stay inside a stuffy ol' room and work all day long."

Deborah placed the stack of sateen, silk, and broadcloth on the bed and then turned back to Torie. "It's our livelihood. And there's a lot of satisfaction in creating a lovely gown that makes a person happy. Or to be able to alter clothes—like yours and your mother's—so that you can enjoy what you already own without having to replace perfectly good clothes."

"We can buy anything we want," Torie boasted.

A soft tapping interrupted their conversation, and before Deborah could make a move, Torie turned and bounded into the other room to answer the knock.

"Ridge! What do you want?" Torie asked crossly.

Deborah stiffened, awaiting his reply.

"I just wanted to see if Miss Holt needed anything."

"Stop acting like a knight in shining armor, Ridge. You're just trying to court her."

Deborah winced. She was grateful that she had remained in the sewing room.

"Listen to me, Victoria." His stern voice filled the adjoining room. "Mother and Father may put up with your sassiness, but *I* don't intend to. Unless you change your attitude, you're going to get a spanking that's long overdue."

"From who?"

"From me! And if you don't think I mean what I

27

say, just keep on pushing. You'll soon find out that I don't back down as easily as Mother and Father."

"Hmph! You're just trying to move back in and take over," Torie retorted. "Why did you come to California anyway?"

A tense silence followed, one that made Deborah anxious and uncomfortable. How could Torie be so cruel?

"Because I had hoped that *home* might be different now," his voice was low. "But I see that nothing has changed."

The door slammed and there was another moment of silence before Torie's sharp little laugh filled the air. Deborah frowned, absently shaking her head. Her big brother was right! She needed discipline.

Deborah lifted a hand to her brow, as though her trailing fingers could somehow erase her frenzied thoughts. She was in this house to work as a seamstress, nothing more. She couldn't allow herself to get entangled in the family arguments.

"Guess you heard that?" Torie stood in the doorway. The glint of mischievous triumph in her eyes was denied by the white line around her mouth, the tremulous lips. "He couldn't get along with Mother before so he went to live in Texas. Now he wants to come out here and boss everybody around."

Deborah pressed her lips together as she busied herself with straightening the small room. She would not voice an opinion—she wouldn't! Yet she found herself thinking that if she had an older brother she certainly would not treat him as Torie had.

"I never had a brother or sister," she said, her voice soft and wistful. "I always wished for both, or just one. Maybe you don't agree with me now, but someday you might be glad you have a brother."

"No, I won't be. I don't like Ridge. He's too bossy."

Deborah resisted the impulse to say more. She turned back to her unpacking, ignoring Torie in the hope that she would take the hint and leave. But she lingered, snooping through the material and patterns.

"Maybe I will let you teach me how to sew on buttons," she conceded. "It's better than doing *nothing* all day long."

"All right," Deborah forced herself to be friendly. 'Maybe I could even teach you to embroider."

Torie's eyes widened. "You mean put fancy little designs on material? Like this?" Torie pointed to her dress.

"I doubt that we could do *that* well," she laughed. "But we could do something basic, perhaps."

"Okay," she said. "I'd like that."

"Victoria? *Victoria!*"

Adell's voice brought a sullen frown to Torie's face. "It's my bedtime. See you tomorrow."

She turned and dashed out, slamming the door so loudly that Deborah feared it might topple from the hinges. Deborah took a deep long breath, relieved to be alone at last. She felt as though she had been slowly and carefully dissected by each member of the family.

Wearily, she glanced around her, amazed that she had been able to organize the sewing room to her satisfaction in the midst of Torie's prying eyes. She wandered back into her bedroom and sank down on the bed, far too tense to think about sleeping.

If only she had some entertainment. Perhaps Torie would have a book she could borrow. She had brought her Bible, and would spend time in devotions

29

and prayer in the morning, but now she wanted something light and whimsical.

She got up and hurried across to open the door and peer into the hall, thinking she might slip to Torie's room. But the eyes she met at the end of the hall were dark gray . . . and belonged to a tall, dark-haired man who was slowly walking down toward her room.

Deborah stiffened, resisting a foolish impulse to turn and dart back inside. But it was too late, anyway. He was beside her.

"Are you comfortable here, Miss Holt?"

"Yes, very," she murmured, her bottom lip pinched between her teeth.

"Were you looking for someone?" he asked. His lips quirked as though he were amused by something.

Deborah drew herself up to her full height, unsure why he looked as though he were about to laugh. Feeling defensive, she tilted her dark head back, her green eyes sparkling.

"As a matter of fact, I was thinking of going to Torie's room to see if I could borrow a book," she said briskly. Did he think she was out snooping in the hall? What *did* he think?

"A book?" A dark brow quirked. "Then perhaps you'd rather see our selection of books down in the library. They'd be more suited to your taste than Torie's books, I imagine." Again, the tilt of the lips.

"On second thought, I suddenly feel very tired. Perhaps I'll pass on the reading tonight."

He bowed politely. "Whatever you wish."

"Good night," she said in a clipped tone.

With as much dignity as she could summon, she turned and entered her room and closed the door without a backward glance. A soft chuckle filled the hallway beyond the door, before muffled steps whispered down the hallway.

Why was he laughing? she wondered, her cheeks burning. Did he know how nervous he made her? Probably! No doubt, he had that effect on all women.

She leaned against the door, her heart racing with anger and humiliation—and something more. She had an uncomfortable feeling there were going to be more problems here than she imagined. And Ridge Farrington was definitely one of them.

CHAPTER 3

MARGARITA SURPRISED DEBORAH the next morning with a tray of fresh orange juice and rich, dark coffee. After a good night's rest, Deborah suddenly felt more equipped to cope with the challenges at Cimarron.

She padded barefoot across the carpet to lift the window for a breath of fresh country air. The sweet fragrance of roses and bougainvillaea drifted into the room, and she took a deep breath, delighting in their fragrance. She parted the curtain and stared out at her new surroundings.

Below her, the veranda was deserted. A bee droned over the rose bush, its steady whir the only sound in the golden morning. As she squinted through the bright sunlight, she glimpsed a rider on a magnificent black stallion, cantering up the driveway. He seemed to be an extension of the horse, his movements were so graceful, with a wide brimmed black hat shading his face. Though dressed like a ranch hand, there was no mistaking the identity of the rider. It was Ridge

Farrington. As he neared the arched entrance, he urged the horse into a gallop, and the two thundered up the drive at break-neck speed.

A vaquero at heart, she thought, despite the time he had spent away from ranch life. *Why had he left his family?* she wondered, remembering the conversation she had overheard the night before between Torie and Ridge.

She recalled his words: *I had hoped that home might be different now. But nothing has changed. . . .*

Did he leave home to escape Torie and Adell?

She watched him disappear around the house, unable to drag her eyes from man and horse. It would do her no good to be curious about him, she reminded herself. Adell would never allow it.

She dropped the curtain, but she continued to stand before the window, absorbing the tranquility of the country air.

"Father, you would have loved it here," she whispered softly, remembering again the dream, Jim Holt's dream.

She sighed, squeezing her dark lashes together in an effort to hold back the tears. Jim Holt had wanted a ranch, more than anything in the world. In California he hoped to obtain a land grant and start his ranch, where he and his family could have fruit orchards and a vegetable garden, and horses . . .

Her dark lashes parted, her battle not to cry, lost. Tears shimmered in her green eyes, making them sparkle like polished emeralds. She sniffed, as a tear slid down her rounded cheek, and she lifted the curtain again to stare out at Cimarron.

In a strange way, she had been blessed, she thought. She was getting room and board at one of the finest ranches in southern California, and the work wouldn't be hard. She had been sewing for years. Certainly the alterations would not be difficult. Why hadn't she seen the blessing rather than the hardship?

She would make the most of her time at Cimarron, she decided. She would absorb and enjoy the feeling of ranch life—living out briefly the dream her father had cherished. She would be pleasant to Adell and befriend Torie.

Suddenly, her spirits lifted and she hurried to her wardrobe, choosing her clothes for the day. By the time she dressed and began her work in the sewing room, she was softly humming a favorite hymn.

Adell had already dropped off a blue satin dress with a request to tighten the buttons. Such a simple task, Deborah smiled to herself, touching the gleaming satin with pride. A task that Adell was perfectly capable of doing herself, if not for the fact that she left menial tasks to the "hired help." The corners of Deborah's mouth tilted in an amused grin. Somehow the knowledge that she was only *hired help* failed to offend her now.

The hours slipped away and she was startled when Torie poked her head through the door to announce lunch. She was tempted to order a tray up in an effort to avoid the family, but remembering her vow to win Torie's friendship, she pushed the dress aside and stood, stretching her taut muscles.

"What have you been doing this morning?" she smiled at the sullen girl.

"Nothing." Torie was wearing another fancy dress, an ice blue sateen that belonged at a tea party in San Francisco, rather than in a ranch house miles from town.

As Deborah's eyes drifted over the formal dress, she suddenly realized the sad plight of this child who had been cheated out of the carefree play of youth. No wonder she never smiled.

They wound down the stairway to the formal living room, which was empty, and into the dining room, where only two places were set.

"Mother's gone to one of her meetings," Torie explained, glimpsing Deborah's puzzled face. "And Father is attending another cattle auction."

Deborah nodded, smiling at Margarita as she entered with a platter of enchiladas.

"Ridge and the cowboys are breaking some mustangs," she added dully.

"Oh?" Deborah's dark brows arched curiously. "That would be fun to watch."

Torie looked at Deborah doubtfully as she lifted an enchilada onto her plate, then pushed it idly around with a fork. "I don't see anything fun about that."

"Well, I do. I've always liked horses. I used to ride with a friend back in Kansas." She paused between bites, glancing at Torie's pale skin. "Do you ever go for walks, Torie? I enjoy walking. After sitting for hours over my sewing, a long walk is like a spring tonic. I'll bet there are some wonderful places to walk here."

"Maybe," Torie shrugged.

Deborah finished her enchilada and sipped her iced tea, giving Torie time to think about what she had said. When finally the girl pushed her plate back and glanced cautiously at her, Deborah lifted the napkin to her mouth and stood.

"Want to walk down and watch them work with the mustangs?"

Torie hesitated. "I guess so. I'll show you where the corrals are," she offered, leading the way out the back door into the glaring noon sunlight.

The grounds were well-kept. A courtyard surrounded the back of the house where blood-red roses climbed white trellises, and pink oleanders shaded an old wooden swing. Beyond the courtyard the valley was rich with alfilaria and other grasses, and to the west an orange grove dispelled a sweet citrus odor across the land.

Deborah sighed, feeling the soft tranquility seep into her being. *What a beautiful ranch*, she thought, cupping her palm over her eyes to shade her vision from the blinding sun.

The stable and corrals were set almost a quarter mile from the house, but she could see a cluster of men there and she smiled at Torie. "Well, let's go."

The path was deeply cut from the back yard to the stable, and the dryness of the morning sent the yellow dust spiraling up about the hem of their dresses as they walked along.

"I never go down there," Torie mumbled, her small face puckered as she squinted into the sun.

"Does your mother object?" Deborah asked.

"I don't know. I never asked her. I just don't care about hanging around a stinking old barn, watching cowboys spit tobacco juice while they fool with the horses."

"Oh. Well, maybe it isn't such a good idea," Deborah stopped walking.

"We might as well go," Torie pouted, "since we're already halfway there."

Deborah nodded and they continued on.

Shouts of encouragement rang through the air as Deborah and Torie reached the corral.

The cowboys were lined up around the split rail fence. The shorter men were standing on the wooden watering trough, peering over heads.

As Deborah and Torie approached, Deborah caught a glimpse of dark hooves flying through the air as a black mustang with white blaze shot into the air, it's legs stiffened.

"Ridge is riding!" Torie squealed, grabbing Deborah's arm.

Deborah sidestepped an enthusiastic observer to get a better look at the rider attempting to hang on to the fighting horse. The mustang's hooves tore into the ground, kicking up swirls of yellow dust as he twisted and bucked in an effort to free himself of the determined rider.

Ridge held fast. His dark work shirt and jeans were sprayed with the dust that clung to his bronzed face and dark hair. On the ground, his black felt hat had been smashed under the mustang's pounding hooves. His arm was flailing through the air in an effort to balance himself while his muscles worked beneath the sweat-stained shirt.

A sharp gasp brought Deborah's attention back to Torie. Her little face had turned deathly pale. Deborah placed a comforting hand on the girl's thin shoulder.

"He'll be all right. The cowboys will jump in to help if he doesn't break the horse soon."

Or at least she *hoped* they would! How much more could he take, she wondered, studying the taut face. As she watched, she felt a spark of respect flicker and grow within her while Ridge took the grueling punishment. Her hand tightened on Torie's shoulder as he was pitched higher and higher into the air, his tall body appearing featherlight.

Deborah bit her lip, regretting her foolish suggestion to come watch. Just as her lips parted to insist on returning to the house, the wild hooves relented their useless fight and the horse stopped jumping. He stood, snorting and trembling, one foot pawing the dirt in final protest.

Ridge swung down and walked around to stare the horse in the eye, one hand gently rubbing its lathered neck and chest. He spoke softly to the horse, who occasionally tossed its head. As Ridge continued to speak softly, the horse stopped trembling and watched him quietly.

Ridge grinned at the cowboys, quietly asserting his victory as he stepped up into the saddle once more. The mustang thrust its head down, but when he did so, Ridge held a taut rein, gently touching the horse's gleaming neck as he spoke again. Shifting his weight in the saddle, he urged the horse into a circle around the corral.

"Did you see him?" Torie squealed, tugging Deborah's sleeve. "Ridge broke that wild horse. He *broke* him!"

"Yes," Deborah released her pent-up breath. "He certainly did."

Roberto broke through the exuberant crowd and ducked under the rail. Eyes glowing with respect, he stood by as Ridge sprang down from the saddle.

"He's all yours, Roberto," Ridge panted, slapping him affectionately on the shoulder.

For a moment it appeared that Roberto would throw his arms around Ridge and weep with joy, but instead he danced up and down, shouting his thanks.

"Graçias, graçias!" His shouts were accompanied by laughter and more shouts of congratulations as Ridge bounded out of the ring.

"Well, shall we go?" Deborah turned to Torie, suddenly eager to get away before they were forced to speak with Ridge.

"Ridge!" Torie screamed, ignoring Deborah.

He whirled in surprise, his arm lifted to mop his perspiring brow. At the sight of two females among a company of rowdy males, the dark brows arched quizzically.

Deborah bit her lip, certain he would scold them for standing around the corral where only men stayed. But to her surprise, a slow, wide grin spread over the gleaming face and he bolted to them.

"Ridge, you broke him!" Torie screamed again, still enraptured by what she had witnessed.

He looked down into his sister's uptilted face and nodded. "Well, maybe. Roberto will still have to work with him."

"I didn't know you could do anything like that," Torie said, her admiration apparent in her soft tone and her glowing eyes.

Ridge stared at her for a moment, obviously taken aback by her sudden change of attitude. "You never came to watch before," he grinned, lifting a hand to tug at her limp braid. The dark gray eyes then riveted to Deborah. "How did you manage to drag her out of the house?"

Deborah twisted uncomfortably beneath the penetrating eyes. "Oh, I don't know. We needed some exercise, didn't we?" she glanced at Torie.

"Yes, we needed exercise," Torie agreed. "When are you going to break some more horses? I want to come back to watch."

Ridge laughed, looking back at the subdued horse. "That was the worst one. The boys will get the rest."

Deborah's green eyes flickered over his dusty clothes as she struggled with growing admiration. She turned back to Torie, trying to break the spell he was casting on her.

"Shall we go back now?" she asked, avoiding Ridge's sudden sweeping gaze.

"Yes, do go back and tell Margarita to make fresh lemonade," he said to Torie. "Then if you two will join me on the veranda, I'll tell you more about the horses."

"Okay," Torie brightened, tugging at Deborah's arm.

Deborah forced a little smile and hurried after Torie. The man had a strange affect on her, or perhaps it was just the sense of danger that had sharpened her nerve endings and made her feel all fluttery inside.

As they reached the back door and Torie began to shout for Margarita, Deborah glanced at the stairs, remembering that her work awaited her.

"Torie, I must get back to work," she said lightly. "You and your brother go on and have your lemonade and talk. I'll see you later in the afternoon."

"Why?" Torie whirled toward her, a pout forming on her small face.

"Well, I . . ." she swallowed, thinking. "I need to finish what I'm doing. Your mother may be needing the dress."

Torie thrust her pointed chin in the air. "Now you act like a grown-up again—just when I thought you might be fun. Well, go on. See if I care. You can sit up there in that hot room and work all day and night, I don't care."

She turned and burst into the kitchen, colliding with a shocked Margarita.

All the excitement of the morning suddenly turned to wariness as Deborah dragged herself back up the steps. How was she going to be friends with a child who behaved so badly? Maybe she *couldn't* be friends with her, she thought sadly.

God, show me how to deal with her, she silently prayed as she reached the top step and hurried down the hall to her sewing room.

As she seated herself at the desk and lifted the dress again, her fingers were as leaden as her heart. She forced herself to do her work, trying to push Torie and Ridge from her mind.

A light knock tapped the closed door, and Deborah thrust the needle back into the satin garment and stood up. She crossed the room to open the door, silently wording a firm refusal to Torie. When she opened the door, however, she was looking into a clean, masculine face with smoke gray eyes.

"Won't you join us?" Ridge asked softly. "Margarita prepared cookies and lemonade for *three* ."

"I . . ." she stared into the handsome face, trying to call forth a gracious refusal, but strangely the words died in her throat.

"Surely your work can wait for a few minutes. I'm going to tell stories about wild mustangs." His eyes widened in a comical gesture of enthusiasm.

"Oh, are you?" she laughed softly.

"All right," she nodded. "I'll be right down."

How could she refuse? she thought, closing the door. The sun was shining, birds were singing, and fresh lemonade and cookies sounded wonderful. And Ridge Farrington was waiting, a voice in her brain taunted.

She closed the door and hurried into the adjoining

41

bedroom to freshen up. In the looking glass, she caught the sparkle in her green eyes and the twin spots of color on her cheeks. She enjoyed Ridge's company. He was considerate, kind, and fun. But . . . she sighed, sweeping her dark hair into its neat chignon. She would have to be careful, *very* careful. Ruffling the lace collar of her gray broadcloth, she turned and hurried downstairs.

Ridge's deep voice floated to her from the veranda and she followed the sound, oddly thrilled by the sound of his voice. She pushed the door open and stepped onto the veranda, a slight smile on her face.

Ridge bolted out of his chair and came over to draw up a small settee for Deborah. Torie was sprawled in the swing.

"Thank you," she murmured, smoothing her skirts beneath her as she sat down before a table of sugar cookies and iced lemonade.

"Ridge was telling me about the first people who lived in this valley," Torie beamed. "They were called Shoshonean. They were Indians!"

"Oh?" Deborah glanced at him inquiringly as she sampled a cookie.

"Well, actually, I had been talking about the wild horses that once inhabited all of this land. Then I mentioned they were free to roam the valley here, although the Indian tribes tried to break them and use them for their horses. Then the Spaniards came and established missions and the Indians were subjected to their rule. Of course, everything changed with the Bear Flag Revolution and the American conquest of California."

He paused to sip his lemonade.

"After California became United States territory,

settlers moved out here, lured by stories from trappers about the mild climate and the abundance of land for growing fruits and vegetables."

"Yes," Deborah smiled sadly, "Those were the stories that lured my father here—much later of course." She glanced out across the valley. "All of his life he had heard about California. He seemed to think it was heaven itself," she laughed softly, glancing back at Torie and Ridge. "He sold his mercantile business and hired on with the Southern Pacific. . . ." Her voice drifted away as her dark lashes swept downward. She sat studying the ice in her glass.

"What happened?" Ridge asked.

"They were repairing a piece of track over a ravine. He fell. . . ." She swallowed, trying to push the awful memory from her mind.

"I'm sorry," Ridge's gentle voice broke into her thoughts. She looked into his sympathetic eyes.

"Thank you," she answered. "We have only been in Los Angeles a short time. My mother and I opened a sewing shop to provide some income for ourselves and," she shrugged lightly, "everything has worked out," she finished, forcing a smile in an effort to restore the carefree mood of minutes before.

Ridge shifted in his chair, staring silently cross the valley for a long moment. "You and your mother have been very brave," he glanced back at her. "Not many women could go on with their lives in a strange place, with no man to help them."

"We hadn't enough money to return to Kansas," Deborah replied. "And Mother seemed strangely compelled to live out my father's dream for him." She turned to glance around her, thinking that she, too, was living out a dream this minute, here at Cimarron. But she pressed her lips together, knowing she could not share such personal thoughts with them.

She was suddenly aware that both were watching her curiously. She could feel a blush rising to he cheeks as they continued to stare at her. Leaning forward, she placed her empty glass on the table and stood.

"I must get back to my work," she smiled. "I enjoyed the refreshments. Thank you."

"Er, Miss Holt," Ridge was standing now. "Do you . . . must you go back up to work? Torie was trying to talk me into letting her ride one of the horses before you came down. Would you care to join us?"

Deborah glanced quickly from Ridge to Torie, seeing the shy grin on her face. Torie hadn't seemed interested in riding earlier, but now she suddenly had changed her mind. Horseback riding!

Deborah ached to ride again, recalling fun-filled days back in Kansas. But what would Adell say when she returned from her meeting and found her out riding, rather than working?

"Sorry, but I must decline. Maybe another day when I'm caught up with my work," she added, seeing the disappointment in both faces.

"Why can't you work on those ol' dresses tonight?" Torie whined.

"Torie!" Ridge snapped. "Don't be rude. Another day would be more suitable for me anyway," he said. "I have fences to check this afternoon. Another day?" he repeated softly.

She stared up at the lean, sun-bronzed face, the careless smile, the dark, curls that toppled haphazardly over his brow, as endearing as those of a young boy. Her heart started to beat faster, and she tore her eyes from his face.

"Another day," she agreed, slowly returning his smile.

CHAPTER 4

THE COMING DAYS brought a flurry of activity within the ranch house. Adell was planning to attend a series of meetings promoting women's suffrage in San Francisco, and she was constantly bursting into the sewing room with dresses to be altered.

Ridge and his father were attending cattle sales in Sacramento. Deborah had tried to spend time with Torie, but the work-filled days left her too exhausted for anything more than a game of checkers. Torie had delighted in those games, relishing easy victories when Deborah almost dozed off to sleep, one hand cupping her chin, the other poised over the checkers.

"I'm glad you play checkers," Torie announced one evening after another victory.

"Well," Deborah shook herself awake, "I like playing with you. You're a smart checker player."

A small frown puckered Torie's high brow. "I could be better if I'd had anyone to play with me. Mother's always going to her meetings. Why do you suppose

46

she is so interested in whether women vote or not?'' she demanded angrily.

"That's an important issue, Torie,'' Deborah replied. "I think your mother is brave to get involved.'' *But maybe not so involved that she neglects her daughter,* Deborah thought with a sigh.

"Father never has time for anything but his cattle, or his railroad meetings. Ridge . . .'' her voice trailed away wistfully.

"I'll bet Ridge would play with you.''

Torie shrugged, staring at the board. "I haven't been very nice to him. Listen,'' her eyes widened suddenly. "He's returning tomorrow. Maybe we can plan to go horseback riding after Mother leaves.''

Deborah glanced at her, as they stacked the checkers and put the board away. "I don't want to do anything to displease your mother, Torie.''

"Why?'' Torie pressed. "Why are you so worried about pleasing my mother? You fix her dresses all the time. All those dresses she's taking to San Francisco are ones you worked on.''

"Yes, I know,'' Deborah responded. "I just meant I want to keep everything . . . pleasant.''

"I know what you mean. It's awful when she gets her feathers ruffled.''

Torie and Deborah exchanged glances then burst into laughter. Slowly, Deborah was winning the little girl over and she counted that accomplishment a great blessing.

Initially, everyone at the dining table was pleasant, the next evening. Adell, aflutter with plans for her departure, failed to notice the frequent glances Ridge gave Deborah. Stuart, normally perceptive, was now engrossed in his latest cattle purchase.

47

"Really, Stuart, I do wish you would accompany me on this trip." Adell's sharp tone brought an end to the relaxed dinner. Even Margarita fled from the dining room, all too aware apparently of the danger lurking in that tone of voice.

"I have a stockholders' meeting, Adell. I cannot possibly miss it."

"Yet you never miss a cattle sale!" She glared at him. "Why can't you leave some of the cattle sales to a foreman? Or," she sneered, "do you wish *you* were still a foreman?"

Stuart Farrington's face turned beet-red, and his thin lips twisted in a grim white line.

"Excuse me," he snarled, tossing his snowy napkin in the middle of the herbed chicken.

Ridge heaved a sigh and uncoiled his long frame from the mahogany chair. "Mother, that was unnecessary.".

"Sometimes I think it *is* necessary, Breckenridge. Your father has to be reminded of his obligations to me."

"Thirty years of reminding should be enough, don't you think?" A muscle clenched in Ridge's lean jaw as he turned on his booted heel and strode out of the dining room.

Deborah stared at her plate, wishing she could quietly disappear without being noticed. It was embarrassing to witness a family argument—a family of which she was no part, and an argument she didn't understand.

"I hate it when you two fight!" Torie screamed, knocking her water glass over as she bolted from the chair and ran from the room, her braid flying about her narrow shoulders.

Deborah lifted her water glass, trying to remain impassive as Margarita rushed in to mop up the water.

"Miss Hold, you must take great delight in this," Adell said.

Deborah turned to her, stunned by her words. "I don't know what you mean, Mrs. Farrington."

"Of course you do! You and your mother are so righteous, tending your little shop, telling everyone how your precious God always takes care of you, as though you were some sort of divine angels."

Deborah gasped. What had they said to Adell Farrington? God *had* taken care of them, and they had shared their faith with some of their customers—but never with Adell!

"It disgusts me to see people as pompous as you and your mother," the cold blue eyes bored through Deborah. "Pretending to be so *good*. And then you gloat over others' mistakes."

Deborah could only stare in disbelief as Adell got up and marched out of the room, her head high.

She truly hates us, Deborah thought, staring into space. She and her mother had never gloated over anything, certainly not anyone's misfortunes. Why would Adell say such a thing? What had they ever done to her to make her despise them so? She stared at the empty dining room for a moment then slowly pushed herself out of the chair and wandered out.

When she reached the hall, she found that she could not force herself back up the stairs where she might encounter Adell in the hall. There was a limit to how many times she could hold her tongue!

With Adell's cruel words still ringing through her ears, she had an insane desire to turn and run out the front door, down the long, dark road to home. She would gladly walk every mile of the way, just to escape the Farringtons.

She heaved a sigh, knowing she could not do such a thing. But she would have to walk for a while, gathering a chestful of fresh air to cool down her rising temper.

She sauntered to the front door and peered into the darkness. All was quiet. Obviously everyone had taken refuge in their room.

She stepped onto the cool veranda, breathing deeply of air, perfumed with the lush roses that filled the grounds. Her eyes followed the graveled drive that led down to the arched entrance, and she lifted up her skirts and hurried down the steps and followed the drive, venting her frustration with each step.

"May I join you?"

The soft male voice floating to her through the darkness spun her around. She squinted across the yard, catching a tall silhouette beside a sycamore.

"Oh," her hand darted to her breast, trying to still her fluttering heart. "You frightened me."

"I'm sorry," Ridge said, emerging into a patch of light from the gas lantern that overhung the veranda.

"I was just getting a breath of fresh air," she responded nervously.

"I imagine you needed one!"

She held herself rigid as he walked toward her. She felt small and vulnerable standing in the moonlight, with his mother's harsh words still haunting her. She did not know how to deal with a woman like Adell Farrington, or with this tall, dark stranger who unnerved her more than she cared to admit.

Trying to gather her composure, she turned and stared out into the night, watching the full moon lay silver streamers across the valley. Somewhere in the distance, a coyote directed his lonely howl to the moon, and his eerie cry seemed to touch some special place in her heart. She felt as lonely as that coyote, and she wished with all of her heart that she was back in Los Angeles, back to the cozy comfort of their little apartment.

"Please accept my apology," he said, after staring at her for a long moment. "My mother was very cruel, and the rest of us forgot our manners as well. It must have made you feel very uncomfortable."

He took a step closer, and the light slanted across his bronzed face. "Are we forgiven?" he asked.

"Of course you're forgiven," she replied. "Every family has its problems. . . ." Her voice trailed away, as she thought of her own family. Thank God, their problems had never resembled those of the Farringtons!

She had been reared and nurtured on love and respect for others. It was hard for her to understand a family so filled with bitterness and resentment. As she stared up into his dark face, she realized, suddenly, that Ridge Farrington had missed something very basic, and she felt a twinge of pity.

"I spent four years back East attending college," he said, folding his hands behind him as he started to walk. Automatically, she fell in step with him.

"When I returned, my parents were as miserable as when I left. It tore me apart to see them fighting with each other all the time. So I left again." He sighed, tilting his head back to stare at the moon. "I moved to Texas for a while. I was just getting started in land development when my father called and told me he had bought a ranch in California. It made me sad to

51

think about my parents and sister living so far away. I decided to join them again. But nothing has changed," he shook his head sadly, glancing back at her.

Deborah sensed the deep pain he felt, and she longed to reach out to him, to offer some words of comfort. But she was an outsider, she reminded herself, she couldn't get involved.

"Torie has been doing better, don't you think?" It was the only encouragement she could think to offer. "She's hoping we can ride horses tomorrow."

"You've been good for her," Ridge smiled. "You could be good for me—very good."

His hand reached out, cupping her chin. Deborah froze, her mind spinning. He was about to kiss her, she sensed that. She should yank free of him, run . . .

The moment of hesitation cost her. He closed the distance between them, and his lips dipped down to touch her cheek. She opened her mouth to protest, but suddenly the protest was silenced as his lips brushed hers.

She tried to ignore her strong attraction to him as she jerked her head back, her eyes suddenly blazing. "Don't ever do that again!"

"Why not?" he asked quietly.

"Because . . . you have no right." She turned on her heel and charged back up the path. *Because you're a Farrington*, she had almost said.

When Deborah awoke the next morning, the sun was already high in the sky, trailing golden rays through the lace curtains by her bed.

She opened her eyes and blinked, glancing across at the window, then pushed herself wearily to her elbow to peer around dazedly. She had tossed and turned

52

through most of the night. Finally, at dawn, exhaustion had taken over, obliterating Ridge Farrington from her thoughts.

She pushed the mass of dark hair from her sleepy face and padded barefoot across to the window, wondering what everyone was doing. When she looked down to the veranda, she met the amused eyes of Ridge Farrington. He was leaning against a post, sipping coffee.

With a gasp, she leapt back from the window, her eyes slipping down her gown, her hands raking through her tangled hair. Her cheeks burned with embarrassment as she seized her wrapper and bound it tightly around her narrow waist. Then she dashed to the basin to wash her face.

The sudden tapping on her door made her jump again, sloshing water down her wrapper. "Who is it?"

The door opened and Torie sauntered in. "Sleepy head," she teased. Her small round face held a pleasant expression, and the blue eyes were bright and cheerful.

Deborah stared at her, water dripping from her chin. There was no way she could predict the actions of this odd family. Little did she expect to face a cheerful Torie this morning.

"Ready to go riding?" Torie asked excitedly. Comprehension dawned as Deborah pressed a towel to her face. "Roberto already took Mother into Los Angeles to board the train for San Francisco. Father is at his meeting. There's only you and me and Ridge. We can have a wonderful day without them."

Deborah winced at the girl's bitter referral to her parents.

"You *are* going to ride, aren't you?" Torie rushed

to her side, anxiously touching her arm. "Please say you are! Please don't spoil our one chance for fun."

Deborah turned shocked eyes to her, unaware how much importance Torie had placed on this event. The girl's small face was already paling as she awaited Deborah's answer.

"Of course I'm going to ride with you," she replied. How could she possibly say no, she wondered. "I wouldn't miss it! Now do me a favor and ask Margarita to please prepare some coffee while I dress."

"Okay." Torie beamed with pleasure as she turned and dashed out.

By the time Deborah and Torie reached the stable, Ridge had saddled up the horses and stood waiting, an amused grin softening his dark face.

Deborah felt her cheeks glowing as she recalled her last encounter with him. She sensed he was watching her for her reaction, and she chose not to return his gaze.

"Which one is mine?" Torie squealed, glancing from a small docile mare to a larger bay.

"The mare," he replied, turning back to check the harness. "Have you ever ridden, Deborah?" he called over his shoulder.

"Yes, I have," she replied.

"I thought so. That's why I chose this one for you." He pointed toward the sturdy bay. He was a handsome horse with stockinged feet and a blaze on his forehead.

"He's magnificent," Deborah murmured, hurrying around to stroke the horse's neck.

"What's my horse's name, Ridge?" Torie shouted, scarcely able to contain her excitement.

"Lady. The other one is Midnight. We bought these two horses when we went to Sacramento. They belonged to a rancher and his daughter." He glanced at Torie. "I had you in mind when we bought them."

"You did?" Torie squealed, turning to throw her arms around Ridge in an awkward embrace. "Oh, thank you Ridge!"

Deborah was more reserved with her gratitude, but she favored Ridge with a pleasant smile. It made her happy to know that he was trying to help Torie. Her eyes roamed over Torie's uplifted face, noting the gleam in her eyes. She could scarcely believe the change in the girl over the past week. "Torie, I'm glad you decided you'd enjoy riding," Deborah smiled at her.

"I . . . I've always been afraid of horses," she admitted sheepishly, her eyes lowered.

"Well, you don't have to be afraid today, little one," Ridge was checking the girth under the horse's belly. "I'm putting a lead on the mare, and you'll ride beside me."

"I want to ride by myself," she objected, then fell silent at Ridge's look. "Oh, all right," she conceded, turning back to stroke the little mare's face.

Ridge helped them into the saddles, then led the way out of the stable. Deborah was becoming almost as excited as Torie as she held the reins lightly, feeling the familiar sway of the horse beneath her.

She had missed those carefree days back in Kansas, those afternoons when she and her friends went for rides in the fields just west of town. Now her life was filled with work and there was no time for anything more, it seemed.

Her eyes drifted to the tall, broad-shouldered man

in front of her. He sat erect on his mount, moving with the horse as though he had been born in the saddle. Deborah felt awkward and self-conscious around him now, yet strangely exhilarated. She forced her eyes back to the trail before them. Sunlight spilled over the elderberry bushes, highlighting the lemon-colored blossoms. Just ahead, the poppies on the hillside were like a crimson sea.

The gentle breeze stirring the oaks and cotton-woods ruffled the dark tendrils about her face, and as she took a deep breath, she suddenly felt more alive than she had felt in a very long time.

She glanced across at Torie, who was clinging bravely to the saddlehorn, her placid face tilted toward the sky. Today she was dressed in a simple brown skirt, which was far more becoming than the frilly tea dresses she usually wore.

"We'll ride up to Sunset Point," Ridge said at last, pointing to the distant rise that overlooked another valley.

"Ridge, have you missed ranch life?" Torie asked, in a shy little voice.

Ridge was silent, thinking. Deborah glanced curiously at him.

"Yes, I have, Torie," he sighed. "But I was happy in land development. It's fascinating work, and work I hope to do here."

"Here?" Deborah echoed.

"Yes, here in the valley. I'll show you where when we reach the Point."

The trail wound up a flowered hillside, past mazanita bushes, then widened onto a grassy plateau. Ridge swung down and tethered his mount, then turned to hold the other horses as Torie and Deborah dismounted.

"This is the highest point on the ranch," he said, pointing across the vista. "We can see all the way to Los Angeles from here."

Torie and Deborah picked their way over rocks and gopher holes to the vantage point where Ridge stood. Both gasped when they looked down at the view before them.

Citrus groves, fruit orchards, and grape vineyards created colorful squares, like pieces of a patchwork quilt. Beyond the farming area, the heart of Los Angeles was nestled in a flat basin, and far in the distance, the Pacific Ocean curled against the horizon.

"You see, there's plenty of room for growth up the valley. The original ranches comprised thousands of acres, but now they are being divided into small communities. Settlers need places to build, and I intend to help them."

"Surely you don't intend to carve up this beautiful valley into homesites!" Deborah gasped.

"Why not?"

Her eyes scanned the tranquil valley below them. "Because there are other places for people to build. They can go north to San Francisco."

"They can . . . but like you and me, they like it here."

She stared at him for a long moment, seeing his logic, yet hating to acknowledge it. Her father's wistful voice filled her memory. "Freedom and space for everyone," he had said.

Her eyes scanned the valley below. If the land was carved up in little squares, Los Angeles would one day resemble the towns back East, gobbled up by people.

"Ridge, you're just trying to make a lot of money

like Father," Torie teased, as she skipped back down the hillside to gather a handful of poppies.

Deborah turned and walked over to a flat boulder to sit down. As the wind ruffled her hair, she closed her eyes and drank in the fragrance of wildflowers, citrus groves, vineyards, the sweet tantalizing mixture as native to California as the ocean and sky.

"I see your point," she opened her eyes and looked at him. "I can't blame people for wanting their little place in the country. It's just that . . ."

"I know," he sighed. "It would be nice to keep it this way, but *that* changed everything." He pointed to the railroad tracks bordering the town. At a distance, they were silver ribbons glinting in the bright sunlight. "The railroad has stitched California to the rest of the nation now, and to promote travel on the railroad, the stockholders are publicizing California as a land of eternal spring. I should know. My father is a stockholder."

Deborah nodded, staring thoughtfully into the distance.

"Deborah," Ridge took a deep breath and shoved his hands in his back pockets. "I'm sorry about last night. I shouldn't have kissed you."

She glanced nervously at Torie, wondering if she had heard. The small girl was skipping merrily through a field of poppies, her braid bouncing about her shoulders.

"It's all right," she said, unable to look at him.

"Well, tell me about Kansas. What did you do back there?" He smiled, apparently sensing her desire to change the subject.

"My father owned a mercantile in Kansas City. The store was our lives. Even now I can close my eyes and see the walnut counter and piece goods and I can smell the peppermint candy and saddle soap." A smile spread over her face, deepening the dimple in her right cheek. "At Christmas, I used to wander up and down the aisles, staring at the China dolls and toy soldiers and fancy pocket knives, wishing for one of each."

"Sounds like a wonderful life," Ridge replied.

"My mother had a little sewing room adjoining the main part of the store. She made dresses for the ladies from bolts of material on the counter. It was a good life," she finished softly, glancing at him. He was staring intently at her, a look that suddenly made her uncomfortable.

What was he thinking, she wondered, turning to study the valley again.

"Do I detect a note of nostalgia in your voice?" he finally asked. "Do you miss Kansas?"

"Sometimes. We had to start all over out here. Everything was strange to us. I miss my cousins, and the friends I grew up with. But we'll make it. We always have, we always will."

"You sound very sure about that."

"I am."

He removed his hat and pushed back the mass of dark curls. "You and your mother are very strong. Want to tell me the source of your strength?"

She hesitated, recalling Adell's cruel remark. Did she dare mention her faith? But how could she evade his question?

"God," she replied softly.

"He's my source of strength too," Ridge smiled. "But I'm afraid I don't often acknowledge it."

In a household that seemed so self-centered and

59

unloving, she almost found it difficult to believe that Ridge shared her faith. Then she found herself responding. "Yes, you do," she nodded thoughtfully. "From the beginning, I sensed that you were . . ." She bit her lip, knowing her reply would label the rest of his family.

"Perhaps different from the rest of my family," he agreed. "Unfortunately, I haven't been able to talk to them about God. It's very difficult. . . ."

"I understand. Sometimes family and friends are the hardest to reach."

Torie's approaching footsteps ended their conversation.

"What are you two talking about?" she asked, her small head tilted curiously, a suspicious look in her eye.

"Just family things," Ridge responded.

She glared at them for a moment. "I'm ready to go back now," she said sullenly, hugging the poppies against her chest.

Ridge and Deborah stared at her, wondering what had altered her pleasant mood. "That's a good idea," Deborah replied, "I have work waiting. But this has been wonderful." She looked back at Ridge, her eyes mirroring her appreciation.

"We'll do it again," he said, returning her smile.

"Let's go!" Torie whined, fidgeting from one foot to another.

"Slow down, Torie," Ridge frowned. "We're coming. There's no need to get upset."

Deborah hurried to her horse, perplexed by the change in Torie's behavior. The three rode back to the ranch in silence. Torie's strange mood had overshadowed the glorious morning.

"What were you and Ridge really talking about?" Torie poked her head into the sewing room.

Deborah glanced up from the dress she was mending, startled by Torie's abrupt question.

"When?" she asked as Torie came into the room.

"When I was picking flowers. You know when! You were talking about me, weren't you?"

Deborah laid the dress aside and looked at Torie.

"We were talking about your family."

"What were you saying?" she cried. "You had no right to whisper like that."

"Torie, we were not whispering!"

"What were you saying?" she cried, tears welling in her blue eyes. "I want to know."

Deborah took a deep breath, knowing she must be perfectly honest.

"Your brother wanted to know how my mother and I had been able to manage without my father here," she began softly. "When he questioned our source of strength, I told him we relied on God. He said that God was his source of strength, too. But . . ." she hesitated, choosing her words carefully, "that he had not been able to talk to his family about God."

"I don't understand," Torie looked confused. "What did Ridge mean by that? We've heard about God. Sometimes I believe in Him and sometimes I don't."

Torie's words, and the indifferent manner in which she spoke them, tugged at Deborah's heart.

"You believe in God sometimes," she repeated. "Why?"

"Because of Margarita. She used to tell me stories about the Cross she wears. About the Jesus who died on a Cross. Until Mother stopped her," she added, sauntering around the room.

"Why did your mother stop her?" Deborah asked.

"Mother says intelligent people should make up their own minds about believing in a higher power. She says when I attend school back East that I can study all the religions and decide for myself which one is right for me. Or if I even want to choose one."

Deborah stared at her, amazed. She believed that a child should be nurtured in faith by parents' teachings and examples, not by some stranger who might not have the child's interest at heart.

"Torie, we're free to make a choice about accepting or rejecting God from the time we are old enough to understand."

Then she hesitated, knowing she was treading on dangerous ground by discussing religion if Adell had forbidden it. Still, she could not, in good conscience, keep silent.

"I'm glad I didn't have to wait until I was grown to learn about God," she continued, a warm smile lighting her face. "I grew up memorizing scriptures which have strengthened me during difficult times. And every day of my life I call on God to help me. I . . . don't know what I would do without Him."

She studied the perplexed expression on the child's face, knowing that God could make such a difference in her life.

But she had given her enough to think about. Perhaps they could discuss this another time when Torie was in a more receptive mood.

"I have to go now," Torie said in a quiet voice, as she strolled back toward the door. "I don't think I want to hear any more about religion. It's boring."

Deborah sighed, wondering if she had succeeded or failed in making her point.

"I'll see you at dinner," she said. "Maybe we can play a game afterwards."

Torie shrugged. "Maybe."

CHAPTER 5

"HELLO."

Deborah glanced up from her work to see a clean, freshly dressed Ridge standing in her door, a broad smile on his face.

"Hello," she replied breathlessly, suddenly conscious of her mussed hair and rumpled dress. She had closeted herself in her sewing room, dreading Adell's return only to be informed by a happy Margarita that the Señora would not be returning for another day.

"I came to invite you to dine out with me this evening. You've been working too hard," he glanced at the stack of dresses. "You've earned yourself dinner. What do you say?"

The invitation was tempting, but Deborah knew she must refuse. Her gaze lingered on Ridge's tailored gray suit, crisp white shirt, and the dashing red cravat at his throat. The dark mass of curls was combed neatly in place and a flash of white teeth accented his golden tan.

"I'm sorry, but I can't." She sighed. "Thank you for asking."

"Would you change your mind if we took Torie along?" he persisted.

She glanced up, thinking. Torie had taken her meal in her room the evening before, and had not popped into the sewing room this morning in her usual habit. Deborah regretted the barrier Torie had erected between them, and she longed for an opportunity to penetrate that barrier. But would a trip into Los Angeles for dinner provide the right opportunity? Or would Torie grow even more jealous?

"I don't see anything wrong with my taking you and Torie into town for a pleasant evening," Ridge continued, sensing that she was wavering. "Shall I go ask Torie?"

"Ridge," she laid the dress aside and lifted troubled eyes to him. "Yesterday Torie came in an demanded to know what we were talking about at Sunset Point. I suppose she must have sensed that we were discussing something rather personal—and something that concerned her. The subject of religion came up." She shook her head. "When I told her about God, or rather how I felt about God, she seemed troubled."

Ridge's smile faded, replaced by a look of deep concern. "Mother forbade Margarita to speak of religion to Torie." His dark eyes were filled with sadness as he looked at Deborah. "You see, Mother doesn't believe in God."

"Oh," Deborah heard herself echo as a chill raced down her spine. Adell had seemed so hard and cold and . . . bitter. Ridge's statement explained why.

"How does your father feel?" she asked, remembering the intense man.

Ridge leaned against the doorway and stared across the room. "Father believes in God, but living with Mother has made him a bit cynical about life. Although he rarely speaks of faith, he shook my hand when I told him that I had come to know God. He told me I had made a very wise decision . . . that I would have a happier life. Unfortunately, his prayers for Mother have not been answered. She is . . . a very stubborn woman."

"Perhaps in time," she offered hopefully.

"Perhaps. But to prevent trouble, it might be wise not to say anything more to Torie. I'm hoping that by improving our relationship, I can earn her respect. Then I'll try to talk with her."

Deborah nodded. "Perhaps that is the best way."

"So, what do you think about having dinner with Torie and me this evening? It's going to be a perfect night for a ride in the carriage." The soft breeze floating through the open window confirmed his words.

She glanced wistfully toward the window, eager to escape the cramped sewing room and the stack of dresses.

"How could I refuse?" She laughed softly.

"You couldn't." He touched her arm. "And Torie will be pleased."

"I hope so," she smiled, watching him bound out of the room with a triumphant smile.

She pulled herself up from the chair, pressing a small hand to the base of her spine. Her muscles were sore and rigid from working long hard hours. She wandered over to lift the curtain and gaze out across the fields of Cimarron.

The sun was moving westward, trailing scarlet

ribbons over the valley. There was a quiet peace overhanging Cimarron, a peace that seeped into her very soul. *If only things could be different*, she thought sadly. But she must accept reality. Still, there was no reason she shouldn't enjoy herself just this once. She turned to her wardrobe and flung the door wide, seeking her prettiest dress.

The sun hung suspended on the horizon, bathing the valley in its fiery glow. As the carriage rolled down the countryroad, Toric and Deborah were content to stare out at the landscape, spellbound by the sunset.

Aware of Ridge's disconcerting glances, Deborah nervously adjusted her lacy shawl around her shoulders, and studied the skirt of her blue taffeta dress. The soft indigo brought out the peach blush in her fair skin, and deepened the sparkle in her eyes.

Torie wiggled constantly, unable to contain her enthusiasm. In the past eight months at Cimarron, she had never been taken into town for an evening meal. She bunched the skirt of her green sateen dress in her small gloved hands and glanced inquiringly at Ridge.

"Can we ride horses again tomorrow, Ridge?" she asked pleasantly.

"Sorry, sis. I'm taking some of the ranch hands further up the canyon to build fences. We need more pastureland for the stock Dad and I are buying."

Watching Torie's smile fade, Deborah suddenly had an idea.

"If it wouldn't be too much trouble to stop by my house, I could pick up some knitting skeins or an embroidery hoop. Maybe we could work on a special project, Torie."

Her suggestion was rewarded with a bright smile.

"Oh, could we? Could we stop by her house, Ridge?" she asked breathlessly.

"Of course we could." He offered Deborah a grateful, amused smile.

Deborah had suggested the project with Torie in mind, but now she realized that seeing her mother for even a few minutes would make her very happy. She missed her mother, though Ridge had suddenly made a difference in her life.

As she studied the sea fog rolling in from the Pacific, she let her thoughts linger on Ridge Farrington. She had never met anyone quite like him. She had misjudged him in the beginning, and now she felt guilty about that. Unfortunately, she had leapt to the conclusion that all the Farringtons were alike. But that had been so unfair! Ridge was courteous, considerate, kind—and he shared her faith!

A warm glow suddenly filled her heart. She could not resist glancing at him. The smoky gray eyes met hers and he smiled—a slow, lazy smile that made her heart beat faster. Her smile was brief, self-conscious before she turned to stare out the window again. The outskirts of town loomed just ahead; flower-vined shacks soon gave way to larger, red-roofed adobes. A sense of comfort slipped over Deborah as they entered the town that had become home to her.

"Do you wish to visit your mother before we eat?" Ridge asked.

She nodded, giving him the address.

He relayed the message to the driver as Deborah glanced eagerly at the narrow streets in her neighborhood. They were passing the grocery, the hardware store and livery stable, then turning into her street. The pepper trees cast dark shadows over small shops and houses as the driver yelled to the horses and the carriage rolled to a stop before her door.

"Would you like to come in?" She glanced at Torie and Ridge.

"We'll just wait in the carriage," Ridge replied tactfully. "Since your mother isn't expecting company, we'll call on her another time."

Deborah nodded, grateful for that reply. The driver opened the door and handed her down, and Deborah's eyes flew to the wooden two-story building. Window boxes on the lower story held a cheerful array of geraniums that compensated for the drab wood, sadly in need of paint. Their sign, delicately painted and curlicued, hung over the door, tugging at her heart as she recalled how she and her mother had made it, laboring long and hard over each letter. She lifted her skirt and dashed up to the door, twisting the knob before discovering her mother had already locked up for the night.

Her mother would be upstairs in the kitchen, brewing her nightly pot of tea. Deborah tapped urgently on the narrow door and waited. Steps descended the stairway then finally the door swung back and Maggie Holt peered into the darkness.

"Mother!" Deborah cried, throwing her arms around the frail woman. "You've lost weight," she scolded, pushing back to look at her.

"Deborah!" Tears of joy shimmered in Maggie's hazel eyes as she looked into her daughter's face.

As the hall light slanted over the petite woman, Deborah's heart ached at the sight of her mother. The blond-brown hair was drab and streaked with gray. Her shoulders sagged with weariness.

"Oh, darling, how I've missed you!" Maggie cried,

hugging Deborah against her thin body. "Who's with you?" she asked suddenly, spotting the black-lacquered carriage and the driver standing at attention.

Deborah glanced over her shoulder. "Torie and her brother. I've come to get some supplies. I'm going to teach Torie to embroider."

"Oh." A tiny frown furrowed the woman's high brow as she stepped aside for Deborah to enter the hall. "Do you want to invite them in?"

"No. I'd like for us to speak in private," she smiled.

"Deborah," her mother's arm circled her shoulders, "are you all right? Is Mrs. Farrington working you to pieces?"

"Mother, I'm just fine," Deborah replied reassuringly as they climbed the stairs. "They're treating me very well. In fact, we're on our way to dinner."

Maggie glanced at her daughter, her eyes widening with surprise.

"Ridge—the brother—is a very considerate man. And he's a Christian, Mother!"

"Thank the Lord!" Maggie sighed as they reached the top stair and Maggie lit the gasolier in the dim living room. The tea kettle was singing, it's familiar sound bringing a lump to Deborah's throat. She glanced over the tiny, cluttered apartment, where dresses in various stages of construction were draped over the horsehair sofa and chairs.

"Mother, you're working your fingers to the bone," Deborah said, lifting a heavy satin dress from a chair and adding it to a pile on the worktable.

"I'm fine. Do you have time for tea?"

"No. But we must talk for a minute." She reached for her mother's hand.

70

Maggie's fingers were cold and frail in Deborah's warm palm. "Mother, you must get more rest. Please! We can make it without your working night and day."

"I know," Maggie nodded. "But I have such good customers. It's had for me to say no."

"Say no for *me*, Mother! You're all I have. I can't let you kill yourself simply because you can't say no. Promise me you'll slow down."

Maggie smiled at her daughter as she lifted a hand to smooth her hair back into the chignon at her nape. "All right, Deborah. I'll try. Now tell me about Cimarron."

"It's beautiful." Deborah said after a thoughtful pause. "I've been thinking of Father lately, knowing how much he would have enjoyed a ranch like that." She paused, as her mother nodded. "My room is nice, and Margarita, the cook, prepares wonderful meals. That's why Adell can no longer wear her clothes!"

Maggie nodded, a frown darkening her face. "That woman had no right to demand your services for so long." Her voice trembled as she spoke, but Deborah lifted a hand to silence her.

"Mother, we've always believed that everything works for our good. Remember you taught me to give thanks in all situations? I'm sure some good will come of this. I'm being treated very well, truly I am."

"You seem to be." Her mother studied her carefully. "And you're right, of course. Some good will come of this. Maybe you could think of this as a vacation."

Deborah forced a brave smile. Her work load was hardly a vacation, but it would be best for her mother if she believed that. "It *is* a vacation at the moment," she repeated. "Mrs. Farrington is in San Francisco at

71

a woman's suffrage meeting, so I'm spared her presence for a few days.'' Suddenly she remembered Ridge and Torie and she stood up. "I'd better get the supplies and join Torie and Ridge.''

A perceptive gleam flashed in Maggie's eyes. "How old is this young man?''

Deborah averted her gaze to the chest of drawers, seeking the embroidery hoop. "In his late twenties, I suppose.''

Maggie touched her daughter's arm. "Deborah, be careful.''

Deborah scooped up the hoop and thread then turned back to her mother. "Don't worry. He's only a friend. And he and Torie have been very nice to me. Now I must go,'' she pressed a kiss on the pale cheek. "I love you—and I'll try to get back for a visit soon. Perhaps Torie will insist on another trip into town. She usually gets what she wants!'' She looked briefly over her shoulder, and flew back down the stairs.

"Take care, darling,'' her mother called, waving to her.

When Deborah glanced up from the bottom step, she was relieved to see a cheerful expression on her mother's face.

"I love you, Mother,'' she waved, letting herself out the front door.

"How is she?'' Ridge asked, handing her in the waiting carriage.

"Tired, I'm afraid.'' Deborah settled into the carriage and tried to resume her cheerful expression. But the memory of her mother's weary face lingered in her mind, and her smile was not as bright as before.

She turned toward the window, trying to divert her thoughts by concentrating on the sights and sounds of night life. This frontier town had seemed strange and vastly different to her quiet neighborhood back in Kansas at first. Now, she was beginning to enjoy the variety of people, along with the Spanish flavor of the town.

The evening passed pleasantly with an elegant meal at the Pico Hotel. But as the carriage returned to Cimarron, Deborah noted a dark frown working over Ridge's face. She tried to read his thoughts, and interpret his sudden silence. Finally, she followed his gaze out the window and saw the source of his problem.

Far in the distance, tiny lights flashed at the upper end of the canyon. Undoubtedly, these were the cattle rustlers Roberto had warned him about. She felt danger lurking in the soft summer night, and she suddenly found herself as tense as Ridge appeared to be.

Torie was nestled against her shoulder, drifting off to sleep. Deborah glanced from the still child to Ridge's worried face. It occurred to her that she would worry about him if he were out in the darkness, chasing thieves. She was aware of the growing attraction between Ridge and herself, one she struggled to ignore. But now she found herself thinking about that kiss in the moonlight, and wondering how she would feel if Ridge kissed her again.

The carriage turned into the drive and Ridge broke the silence.

"Mother must be home."

The words brought instant alarm to Deborah as she turned and stared out the window. Lanterns blazed from every window. On the veranda, Adell Farrington was seated in the swing, staring glumly at the approaching carriage.

"Torie, we're home." Deborah shook her lightly. Torie struggled up, yawning, rubbing sleepy eyes, as the carriage came to a halt.

"Welcome home," Ridge called to his mother.

"Thank you," she nodded, the cold eyes creeping over Deborah.

"Mother, we had a grand time," Torie dashed up to the veranda. "We ate in the dining room of the Pico Hotel, and we went to Deborah's house to get embroidery."

"Embroidery?" Adell stared at the items in Deborah's hands.

"I'm going to teach Torie to embroider—when I'm not altering clothes," she quickly added.

"Really, Torie," Adell gave a condescending little smile, "you wouldn't enjoy doing that. And besides," the voice was edged with contempt, "Miss Holt will be much too busy to embroider. The Warrens are coming next week." She looked at Ridge as though the statement held special significance. "We must prepare for them. Incidentally," she glanced back at Deborah, "my best lace cloth needs hemming. I'll drop it by your room in the morning. Sit down, Torie and Ridge. I have some exciting things to tell you about my trip to San Francisco." Adell's voice softened as she looked at her son and daughter.

"Mother, I can't sit now," Ridge replied distractedly. "There's a matter I must look into." At Adell's puzzled frown, Ridge motioned toward the bunkhouse. "It concerns the workers. No need for you to worry."

"I'll say good night, too," Deborah forced herself to be polite. "Thank you for the pleasant evening," she said to Ridge, ignoring Adell's raking stare.

74

"My pleasure," he beamed.

"Good night, Deborah," Torie's little face was radiant with the lingering joy of her evening in town.

"Good night." Adell's tone was clipped and abrupt. The woman was more than a little upset, Deborah thought, despite the fact that she was making an attempt to conceal her irritation from Ridge and Torie.

Deborah's feet were leaden as she dragged herself up the stairs to her room.

Why had she let Ridge talk her into having dinner with him? The situation was hopeless. If she had any notion of ever going to dinner again, she could forget it! Adell had delivered a sharp message to her, one that seemed to have escaped Ridge and Torie. Yet, the meaning was perfectly clear to Deborah.

She did not belong in their world—and she never would.

CHAPTER 6

"Since the economic depression in Europe, gowns are of much cheaper quality, don't you agree?"

Adell was standing in the center of the sewing room, her arms filled with dresses.

"Look at this! It just arrived from Paris and the seams are already raveling." Adell tossed the limp velveteen dress onto the heap on Deborah's bed, then turned back with a perplexed frown. "I don't want to sound like a tyrant, but it appears that you're getting behind in your work."

Deborah followed Adell's critical gaze to the stack of dresses.

"I appreciate your spending time with Torie," Adell's smile was artificial, her tone patronizing, "particularly since I've been away. But now that I'm back, you need not feel compelled to entertain the child. She can be a nuisance at times." Adell sighed, toying with the gold stickpin at her collar.

"I enjoy being with Torie," Deborah replied quietly. "I think she's a delightful little girl."

"Well, nevertheless, you do have a workload here," she countered, "and I'd appreciate it if you'd make a special effort to catch up."

"All right," Deborah pressed her lips together in an effort to hold her tongue.

But as soon as Adell left the room, Deborah jumped to her feet, flinging her work down. She paced the floor angrily, her arms crossed, her green eyes flashing with anger.

Three more weeks, she told herself. *I can endure three more weeks.*

Or could she? The small room seemed to close in on her as she stood glaring at the mountain of work awaiting her. She would be forced to spend day and night in this room in order to finish the sewing. The full impact of her situation hit her, and she suddenly felt the life draining from her.

Wearily, she reached down and lifted the dress from the floor as her eyes made a sweep of the little room. She had to get out; she had to! She wandered out of her room and down to the kitchen where Margarita's warm smile soothed her frayed nerves. Here was one friend, she thought.

"Hello, Margarita," Deborah forced a tired smile.

Margarita's dark eyes took in her sad face and she tapped her shoulder lightly. "It will be all right," she said.

Deborah nodded, staring at the gold cross that Margarita wore. Margarita caught the direction of her eyes and her plump hand reached up to gingerly touch the cross. "This makes life . . . how you say . . . good. Knowing what we know," she added, the dark eyes twinkling. "He will help you."

"Yes. He always does."

"There you are!" Torie burst into the room. Maybe we can ride to Sunset Point when Ridge comes home."

"I'm sorry, Torie, but I have too much work," Deborah sighed.

"*Work?* I hate people who always have to work," Torie cried, running from the room.

"It is hard for you, si?" Margarita asked softly.

Deborah nodded. "She doesn't understand. Incidentally, I'll be taking my meals in my room until I catch up on my work. I don't expect you to deliver a tray," she explained quickly. "I just didn't want you to go to the trouble of setting a place for me at the dining table."

Margarita nodded, a look of sympathy filling her dark eyes.

Beyond Deborah's window, the night was hot and still. She paced the room restlessly, unable to imprison herself any longer. She cracked her door and scanned the empty hall. The wall sconces were lit, but the only other light seeped from beneath Adell's door. Torie's room was dark.

Deborah crept down the hall then hesitated. Detecting no sound below, she eased down the stairs and opened the back door. Gas lamps in the upstairs windows cast a mellow glow into the darkness. The soft night air brought a sigh of relief as she stepped outside, glancing about her.

A freedom she had not felt all day long enveloped her as she made her way down the garden path. Deborah paused, tossing her head back to breathe deeply. The perfume of roses filled her nostrils, and she felt the tautness in her neck slowly relaxing.

Above her, ominous clouds curtained a half moon. Only a handful of stars offered pinpoints of light.

Dispensing an impulse to turn back, she sauntered on, taking the path to the stable. As her eyes searched the darkness, she caught a movement in the shadows. Her steps slowed as the sound of muted voices drifted to her.

She squinted down the path, watching shadows moving quietly about the corral, shadows that became human forms. Quickly, she turned from the path and darted under an oak. Suddenly, a pair of hands captured her shoulders, and she whirled, wide-eyed, a scream rising in her throat.

"Deborah, it's only me," Ridge was looking down at her. Beneath a low felt hat, his eyes seemed even blacker than the night. Only the flash of his white teeth offset the darkness of eyes and clothes.

Her gaze dropped to his black shirt and pants then rose questioningly to his face again. He was dressed like a vaquero, a fact which puzzled her completely. Behind her, she could hear the men's voices mingling in hushed, apprehensive tones.

"What's going on, Ridge?" She turned to look at the knot of men. One now hoisted a lantern, while the others led saddled horses from the stable. All were dressed in dark clothing.

Ridge hesitated, his hands tightening on her shoulders. "We're going to set a trap for some cattle rustlers who are slipping in at night."

"Oh, Ridge." Her eyes widened. "That sounds dangerous. Please be careful!"

"You're not to worry." His thumbs gently caressed her shoulders. "But Deborah I must ask you not to walk alone at night—not until we catch these thieves."

She nodded, glancing back at the stables.

"Now I'm going to watch you until you're back in the house," Ridge continued. "Go—and please stay inside."

Before she could leave, his hands lifted to cup her face, tilting it back. Gently his mouth closed over hers in a kiss that left her breathless.

"Go," he said, "before I forget my manners and kiss you as a true vaquero kisses his lady love in the moonlight!"

Deborah gave him a brief startled smile and hurried back up the path. Her heart was pounding erratically by the time she reached the back door, and she was uncertain whether it was the kiss, or the sense of impending danger, that had excited her.

She eased open the back door then hesitated. The hall was still deserted. Lifting her skirts above her ankles, she flew up the stairs to her room.

There, she prowled again, more restless than ever. Occasionally, she wandered to the window to stare out into the darkness, searching the meadows, then the road, for riders. But she could see nothing.

She forced herself to undress and prepare for bed, but once she extinguished the lantern and stretched out on the feather mattress, she lay wide-eyed, staring blankly at the ceiling.

Her mind drifted back to Ridge and the men. They were on a dangerous mission, she was fully aware of that. Did Stuart Farrington know what was going on? Did Adell?

Absently, she lifted a hand to touch her lips, recalling the kiss that had left her stunned. She loved Ridge! No matter how hard she tried to convince herself otherwise, she could no longer deny the truth. She loved him.

"Protect him, God," she whispered into the darkness. "Please protect him."

Eventually she dozed, but her sleep was disturbed by nightmares of outlaws and gunfire. Once she bolted upright in her bed, her breasts heaving, her body covered with perspiration as a nightmare of Ridge, alone and dying, filled her mind.

She strained her ears for distant gunfire, but she heard only the trill of a night bird, which seemed to accent the tense silence even more.

She threw the covers aside and crept back to the window, staring for a long time into the black night. Finally, she forced herself back to bed with the knowledge that Ridge and his men were all right. If not, the household would already have been alerted.

Later, voices beneath her window penetrated her half-sleep. She dragged herself out of bed and stumbled, bleary-eyed, to the window to peer out.

Dawn was breaking in the east, illuminating the shadows across the valley. Two men, dressed in black, were leaning against a fence post, sipping coffee.

Relief washed over her at the sight of the men. If these men were back, surely Ridge, too, had returned safely.

She dressed quickly and hurried down to the kitchen. Ridge and Juan stood by the coffee pot, talking quietly. At the sound of her steps, they whirled, casting cautious glances over their shoulders.

"Good morning." She smiled at the tense men.

Juan merely grunted a reply, his leather face taut with the drama of the night. Glancing at Ridge, Juan took his coffee cup and wandered out the back door.

"Any luck?" she asked softly.

"None," Ridge sighed, pouring her a cup of coffee. His lean jaw held the shadow of a beard, and his eyes were hollow and bloodshot.

"You didn't sleep at all, did you?"she asked gently.

He shook his head. "They never came. And that bothers me." A muscle in his jaw clenched as he lifted a hand to sweep his dark, tousled hair from his forehead.

"Maybe you've scared them off for good," she suggested.

"Maybe," he frowned, placing his empty cup on the cabinet. "I'll see you later," he said wearily, offering her a half-hearted smile as he turned and left the kitchen.

Deborah put the last stitch in a hem, then broke the thread with aching fingers and folded the dress over the bed. As she dragged herself from the chair, her petticoats and long skirt seemed to weigh her body down. In a burst of frustration, she lifted her long skirt and yanked her petticoats off. Then she stood before the window, absorbing the hot stale air.

She couldn't decide if the heat was more unbearable with the window open or closed. She glanced over her shoulder at the pile of dresses and her temper began to flare. Sometime during the course of the day, she had made up her mind to grit her teeth and tackle the work load until it was finished. Stubbornly, she had resolved not to let Adell get the best of her.

But the oppressing heat, poor lighting in the room, and sore fingers from needle pricks were gnawing at her good intentions. She wandered into her bedroom and threw herself across the bed, thinking. By closeting herself in her room, suffering like a servant, she was doing exactly as Adell wished. This way, she could not possibly do her best work, and, if she didn't, Adell might instigate some form of revenge.

She sat up on the bed, wearily pushing strands of damp hair from her face. Her eyes drifted to the porcelain basin filled with water. She would bathe, change clothes, and join the family for dinner! She would *not* be bullied by a woman who worked toward equality for women in terms of voting, but insisted on violating the rights of those in her own household. Even her own daughter's!

New energy flowed through Deborah as she bathed and dressed for dinner, selecting the soft, green satin she had worn on the day of her arrival.

All eyes turned to Deborah as she entered the dining room, murmuring an apology for being late for dinner. Margarita scurried to get another place setting. Ridge, appearing rested, came quickly to his feet. His eyes flickered over her, glowing their approval as he hurried to pull her chair back.

"Thank you," Deborah averted her gaze to Torie, seated to her right. The child responded with a half-hearted smile then returned to picking at her food.

"As I was saying," Adell continued, "we have encountered so much prejudice over women voting."

"What do you think, Miss Holt?" Ridge asked suddenly. "Should women vote?"

Deborah looked up startled, the napkin she was spreading in her lap poised in midair. "I . . ." she glanced around the table. All eyes were trained on her, each registering a different form of curiosity. "I think so." She swallowed. "If we're intelligent enough to run homes and rear children, why not?"

"Exactly!" Adell nodded her silver head, a hint of

respect, however begrudging, surfacing in her blue eyes.

"Could we talk about something else?" Torie whined, dropping her fork onto her plate. "I'm tired of hearing about San Francisco and all those meetings. While you were gone, we watched Ridge break a horse," she announced.

"You *what?*" Adell gasped.

"Deborah and I went down to the corrals and watched Ridge break that mustang. It was fun!"

Deborah squirmed, staring at her food and wishing she had not left the sewing room after all.

"I've been asking Torie to come down and see the horses," Ridge filled the awkward silence. "Miss Holt was kind enough to accompany her."

The protruding eyes shot to Ridge. "She went down there among all of those cowboys who spit tobacco and use profanity." Adell was outraged. "You know I don't want Victoria down there! I'll not allow that again, Victoria!"

"Oh, Mother," Torie protested. "You just want me to sit in this hot, stuffy house all day and do nothing, and I *hate* it! I thought that Deborah would teach me to embroider, like she promised, but now all she does is sew on your old dresses."

Stuart Farrington cleared his throat. "Could we please refrain from another disagreement? I'm certain Miss Holt has the impression that all we do is fuss and fight."

The command was threaded with steel, but the dark eyes that rested on Deborah held an unspoken apology. Adell glanced curiously at him, anger flushing her face.

"Ridge," he shifted his attention to his son, still

84

dressed in working clothes, "how did the upper end of that canyon look to you?"

Ridge hesitated, staring at his food. "I need to speak with you about that canyon. Later," he added, his eyes thoughtful as he looked down the table to his father.

"While I was in San Francisco, I saw a house similar to the one we had in Santa Fe," Adell said. "It made me terribly homesick, Stuart." She folded her napkin and stared at him, "I want to have this house redone. I hate Spanish architecture."

"We had a beautiful house in Santa Fe," Torie said to Deborah. "It had Greek columns and was three stories tall. All my friends envied me."

"If you'll excuse me," Ridge pushed his chair back and stood, "I think I'll sit on the veranda for a spell. Miss Holt, are you almost finished?" He indicated her food, scarcely touched. Deborah was grateful for an opportunity to escape.

"Yes, thank you. It was delicious."

Torie jumped to her feet, following Ridge and Deborah from the room. "Want to play checkers, Deborah?"

"Maybe she would prefer to sit on the veranda, Torie," Ridge said.

"Can we play a little bit later?" Deborah touched Torie's arm.

"I'll finish reading my novel," Torie sighed. "Will you come get me when you're ready to play checkers?"

"Of course I will. I won't be long," she called after Torie, as the girl raced up the stairs.

"You must think we behave like heathens," Ridge said, as they stepped onto the cool veranda.

85

She glanced at him, wondering how to reply. "No, of course I don't think that. All families have their disagreements."

Ridge was silent. He shoved his hands deep in his pockets and stared up at the silver moon, riding low in the night sky.

"Mother is so . . . difficult. Sometimes I wonder how my father manages to hold on. I suppose he feels there is nothing else he can do."

Deborah searched her mind for the right words but found none. What he had said was true. She sensed that Stuart Farrington was capable of warmth and tenderness, but his years with Adell seemed to have turned him into a silent, brooding man.

"My mother's family owned one of the largest ranches in New Mexico. Dad was their foreman. As long as they both live, she'll never allow him to forget that he came from poverty, and that without her money and influence, he might still be a foreman. But he would be the best anywhere," he added softly.

Deborah nodded sympathetically. She followed his gaze out across the moonlit meadow where the soft nicker of horses and the lazy bawl of cattle provided a relaxing background for their troubled thoughts.

"Deborah," he turned to look at her, "I'm very attracted to you. I've never met anyone quite like you."

Deborah's eyes widened as she stared at him, sensing his words were sincere.

"In some ways, we hardly know each other, and yet, I feel I've known you all my life. I've never asked before, but is there a man in your life? If so, I don't think I want to know about him. I don't want to think of you with . . . anyone else."

"There's no other man," she said. "There hasn't been time. There still isn't."

"I'm glad there isn't someone else," he said, reaching for her hand. "I don't know how it's possible that someone hasn't married you, but I thank God for it."

"Ridge, please." She tried to pull her hand from his. "This is neither the time nor the place . . ."

"Probably not. But it may be the *only* time and place . . ."

Slowly, he lowered his head and kissed her, a sweet, tender kiss that brought her arms around his shoulders. Deborah knew there could be no future with Ridge Farrington, but she could not resist a fleeting moment in his arms.

When he released her, her eyes were troubled as she stared into his face.

Ridge Farrington had stolen her heart, there was no denying it. Still, she fought against this attraction that had been doomed from the beginning.

Ridge sensed her confusion and stepped back from her.

"I won't push you," he said. "But I do care for you. Very much."

Deborah nodded mutely, gathering up her skirts to hurry inside. Ridge lingered on the veranda, staring after her.

Her mind spinning, she walked down the hallway and turned up the stairs.

A slight rustle behind her made her glance over her shoulder. She caught a glimpse of Adell's silver head as she swept into the parlor and softly closed the door.

Deborah froze in her tracks, her hands gripping the

bannister to support her weak knees. She swallowed, staring at the window that overlooked the veranda.

Had Adell stood before that window minutes before?

And if so, how much had she seen—and heard?

CHAPTER 7

THE ANSWER TO THAT QUESTION came early the next morning when Adell appeared in her doorway, her face grim, her eyes filled with contempt.

"I think we need to have a little talk, Miss Holt," she said.

"Certainly," Deborah consented, silently praying for strength.

"You came here as my seamstress. Nothing more! I do hope you keep that uppermost in your mind."

"Concerning Torie?" Deborah asked, laying her sewing aside. She forced herself to look the woman straight in the eye, hoping to prove she had nothing to hide.

"And Breckenridge as well." She walked into the room, glancing at the mound of work still uncompleted. "I think I would be doing you an injustice if I did not warn you of Breckenridge's carelessness with his . . . affections."

"What do you mean, Mrs. Farrington?" Deborah asked frankly.

"Breckenridge is prone to—how shall I say this?—toy with womens' affections. Most women realize he is only teasing and are smart enough not to take him seriously. Those who *do* end up getting hurt."

Deborah had expected a stiff reprimand, but she was unprepared for this kind of attack. The words she had spoken against Ridge left Deborah speechless. As their meaning registered, Deborah felt the blood rushing to her cheeks, yet she forced herself to keep her head up and meet Adell's challenging stare.

"Mrs. Farrington, Ridge claims to be attracted to me. I won't deny that," Deborah replied. "But I trust you will credit me with the ability to judge for myself if he is sincere, or if he is not."

Adell's cold blue eyes raked over Deborah, as though ferreting any hidden secrets. "Perhaps you are more perceptive than I thought," she finally replied. "Now I'll let you get back to your work." She then swept out of the room.

Deborah stared at the closed door, her hands shaking in her lap. Her throat felt dry and tight; she was on the brink of tears. She knew, of course, what the spiteful woman was trying to do. She should have expected it. And yet . . .

Deborah leaned back in the chair, suddenly weak from this confrontation. And yet what if she were telling the truth? What if Ridge were only toying with her? But no, he wouldn't. He was a man of her faith, a man of God. And Adell was cruel and selfish. How could she believe anything the woman said or did, knowing how she resented her and her mother?

Deborah turned back to her sewing, trying to dismiss the hateful words, but they lingered in her memory, dominating all other thoughts. She avoided lunching with the family and even asked Margarita to send up a dinner tray. When Torie came to check on her, she pleaded a headache. Her excuses to Ridge, however, were less convincing.

"Why are you staying in your room?" he asked, when she answered his persistent knock.

Deborah looked away wishing her honest nature would prevail, forcing her to tell him what really bothered her. But the words faltered on her lips as she thought of Adell.

"A headache," she replied. Why couldn't she open her heart to him? Did she fear Adell's cruel words held a seed of truth?

"I'm sorry," the dark eyes mirrored his regret. "Won't you come down for just a few minutes? A walk in the garden might clear your head."

Or confuse me even more, she thought. "I'm planning to retire early," she answered, still not looking into his eyes, trying to silence the erratic thump of her heart.

"Then I'll say good night," he sighed. "I'm leaving for San Francisco early in the morning, but I'll return in a few days. Perhaps then we can have dinner in town again?"

"Perhaps," she shrugged. This wasn't like her. Why couldn't she be straightforward with him? If only she weren't so tired, so confused.

When he lingered in the doorway, she forced herself to wish him a brisk good evening and close the door. As his footsteps echoed down the hall, she dropped her throbbing head in her hands, fighting her growing attraction to Ridge Farrington.

"Oh, God," she prayed softly, "what have I done? I—I can't feel anything for him. I can't!"

But her words of distress were answered with an inexplicable loneliness the next day as she walked down the empty hall and realized, with a sinking heart, that he was gone. She threw herself into her work, turning out garments with lightning speed. By midafternoon of the following day, she could see the bottom of the stack. Even though her body ached from the grueling torture it had endured for hours on end, Deborah experienced a deep relief that buoyed her spirits once more.

She sought Torie out, needing a brisk walk to ease the ache in her muscles and clear her head. Torie seemed delighted to go. Deborah realized that she, too, was eager for exercise and companionship.

"Why do you believe in God?" Torie asked abruptly as they were strolling through a meadow of wildflowers.

The question caught Deborah unprepared for a moment, since the words seemed out of character with Torie's usual rambling conversation.

Deborah considered her question, glancing out across the landscape, seeing before her a natural beauty that exceeded man's own ability.

"Look at the mountains in the distance, Torie," Deborah pointed. "Think of the sunset and sunrise, the moon set in a galaxy of stars. Someone far greater than you and I created all this. Genesis, the first book of the Bible, describes the creation of the world in such an orderly pattern that I have no doubt an infinite Being, far more powerful than we can comprehend, made our world. And then," she glanced at the path before them, "I believe in Him because I feel Him in my soul. I feel Him when I'm happy or lonely or frightened. He's always there to comfort and sustain me."

Torie was silent for a moment. "Do you have a Bible?" She glanced up at Deborah.

She hesitated, knowing that Adell would disapprove of her lending Torie a Bible, yet how could she refuse? It might be the best opportunity Torie would have to learn about God.

"Yes, I have a Bible in my room," she answered. "I know your mother would object to your reading it, but I believe every person should be allowed to hear about God and His Son."

Torie nodded. "I won't tell her I'm reading it."

Torie's words filled Deborah with sadness. She couldn't imagine a woman withholding a Bible from her child.

The girl was strangely quiet as they returned to the house. Adell was waiting for them on the veranda.

"I've asked Margarita to prepare a light meal," she announced. "Since the men are away for the evening, we can have a sparse meal, for a change." Her gaze held Deborah's. "Could you sit for a minute, Deborah? I'd like to discuss the dresses we'll be needing when our guests arrive."

"Of course," Deborah settled into a chair beside her.

"I'm going upstairs," Torie tossed her head back and glanced at Deborah. "Where is that book you're lending me?"

Deborah stiffened, wishing they did not have to sneak around Adell. "In the drawer of my nightstand," she replied, glancing at Adell who seemed to have her mind on other matters.

"Deborah, I want to say that I'm pleased with your work," she began. "You are a very good seamstress."

"Thank you," Deborah murmured, startled by the compliment.

"I won't be burdening you with more dresses." A hint of a smile tugged at Adell's stiff lips. "If you can just complete what's already in the sewing room, we'll have enough clothes."

"Of course,' Deborah replied quickly. She could scarcely believe the woman was not increasing her work load. Her hopes soared at the possibility of being able to finish her work and return home.

"Good," Adell settled back in her chair to direct her gaze across the green meadows. "I thought we should discuss this while it's on my mind. When Ridge returns, we'll be engrossed in the subject of politics."

"Politics?" Deborah couldn't resist asking.

"Yes. Didn't you know that Ridge is planning to enter politics? He'll make an excellent statesman, don't you think?"

Before Deborah could comment, Adell continued smoothly. "If you'll forgive my saying so, Deborah, this was another reason I tried to discourage you from entertaining any romantic notions about him. While his little flirtations are harmless, he *is* terribly ambitious. Any serious romance on his part will be reserved for a woman from a prominent family—one known in political circles. That's a rather cruel approach, isn't it?" A patronizing smile curved her thin lips. "But, unfortunately, it's the way of politics."

Deborah swallowed, unable to absorb the shock of Adell's announcement. Then, slowly, the words and their meaning registered. The pleasant rapport she thought she was building with Adell suddenly tumbled. She turned bleak eyes to the valley, trying to collect her thoughts, while a deep ache filled her heart.

Why hadn't Ridge told her he was going into politics? Because he knew she was not suited for the political world, the answer came. Nor did she want to be a part of it. Perhaps Adell was right. Perhaps he was not interested in her after all.

She forced herself out of the chair and glanced down at Adell, her chin lifted bravely. "Well, I must get back to work. See you at dinner." Her voice betrayed none of her torment.

Dazed, she hurried up the stairs to her room. Once she reached the second story, however, she turned toward Torie's room. She needed someone to help her sort out her thoughts. There was a chance Torie could shed some light on this.

She knocked softly on Torie's door then called to her. The door cracked and Torie peered out cautiously. "Oh, it's you," Torie smiled, opening the door wider. "Come on in."

"I can't just now, but I wanted to ask you something." Deborah forced a smile and then hesitated. "Torie, I was just wondering about something I overheard." She bit her lip, feeling awkward about asking Torie something concerning Ridge.

"Well, what is it?" Torie shifted from one foot to the other, waiting.

"Is Ridge planning to go into politics?"

"Maybe." Torie shrugged. "He and Mother were talking about it the other day. Yes," she nodded thoughtfully. "Probably. Why?"

"I was just wondering, just curious. Well," she said almost too brightly, "I must go to work. There's lots to be done."

She turned and, after a few calm steps, dashed to her room, locking the door behind her. She sank onto her bed and stared blindly at the ceiling.

In all their conversations, Ridge had never once mentioned political aspirations. If this were his goal, why had he not told her? And if he had not been forthright about his political career, how could she believe anything else . . . like his foolish claim that he cared for her?

She stretched out on the bed, allowing the tears to trickle down her cheeks as she struggled with reality. She had known all along that there was no hope for her love for Ridge. He must have known that too. Yet, he had encouraged her affections.

She lifted a hand to dab impatiently at her wet cheeks. This was merely schoolgirl fascination, she told herself. She had let her heart overrule her common sense.

"It's over," she said to the quiet room. "I'll not talk with him again."

But how could she avoid him for another two weeks?

She turned on her side and stared at the open drawer of her dressing table. If there was any consolation to her miserable association with the Farringtons, it was the opportunity to tell Torie about God. For that she should be thankful.

She forced herself up, wiping the tears from her face as she returned to her sewing.

I will learn to accept this in time, she thought dully. But her heart was as heavy as stone, and she felt old beyond her years.

Ridge had gone to his bunkhouse, troubled and depressed. Deborah Holt had haunted him through every hour of his stay in San Francisco. He had known many women in his life, but no woman had taken hold of his mind and heart as she had. He had been so eager to return to Cimarron that he had almost botched an important cattle sale. Upon his return, however, he had discovered a change in Deborah. She was evasive, cool, indifferent. He had been too stunned to analyze the source of the problem, but he knew it was one that must be dealt with—after he got some rest.

He had finally begun to drift off to sleep, when a strong hand gently shook his shoulder. He blinked, and focused sleepy eyes on Juan's troubled face.

"Wake up, Señor," he whispered. "We have trouble. The guard has spotted riders up the canyon near the cattle."

Ridge blinked at him, remembering that a fiesta in town had claimed most of the men who usually spent a night at the bunk house. But there was no time to worry over their absence, he decided, grateful at least to have the faithful Juan at his side.

"The horses are already saddled," Juan said, his spurs jingling softly as he moved about the room, methodically loading the rifles while Ridge dressed.

Neither spoke again as they left the bunk house and raced down to the stable. Only Roberto waited with the horses at the corral. Ridge tried to conceal his growing apprehension at the realization that he had only two men to go with him as they mounted the horses and cantered down the back trail to the canyon.

The land was cloaked in darkness. Only a thin shaft of moonlight highlighted the distant foothills.

Every muscle in Ridge's body was taut with the sense of danger that awaited them. He studied the dim trail, wondering if he had acted too impulsively. How many men would they discover there? How many could the three of them fight off?

A breeze rattled the chaparral, gently stirring the clouds overhead as the men approached the crest of the foothill. A familiar whistle reached their ears, the signal from the guard. They yanked their horses to a halt and swung down.

Ignacio, the guard, slipped down the path to meet them. He was a strong young man in his early twenties.

"They are just below us," he whispered. "They're camped along the eastern ridge by the stream." There was no tremor to his voice, no fear; only quiet strength and a look of eagerness in his dark glowing eyes.

Ridge complimented himself on choosing Ignacio as his guard. "How many are down there?" he asked, turning to squint through the dark pines.

"Six," Ignacio replied. "Perhaps if we surprise them . . ."

Ridge nodded, glancing back at Juan and Roberto. "It's the only way we can hope to capture them. Bring your rifles, but there is to be no shooting unless in self defense."

Overhead, the clouds continued to drift until the moon came into view, spraying silver across the foothills. The men knelt to remove their spurs, then turned and crept quietly down the side of the hill, down to the floor of the canyon.

Deborah was awakened by hoarse shouts beneath her bedroom window, shouts that rang with alarm. She leapt out of bed, pulling her wrapper about her as she stumbled through the darkness to the window.

Below her, Juan and Roberto stood on the veranda with Stuart Farrington, who was dressed in a satin robe, hoisting a flickering lantern. Beneath its yellow glow, all three faces were clenched with terror. Juan's and Roberto's clothing was torn and dusty. Roberto's shoulder was bleeding.

Deborah gasped, her eyes widening on the circle of red that was spreading across Roberto's shirt. Gently, she lifted the window, too eager to discover what was wrong to feel guilty about eavesdropping.

". . . and then we hemmed them up in the canyon," Juan was explaining. "They started shooting at us, and then all of them made a run for their horses. We tried to follow, but they got away. All except one." He hesitated, the dark eyes filled with worry. "Your son went after him."

"What?" Stuart shouted. "You ran off and left him?"

"No, Señor!" Roberto clutched his bleeding shoulder. "We went after him, but we lost them further up the trail. Then . . ." He broke off, darting a desperate look at Juan.

Juan lowered his head, his shoulders heaving in a deep sigh. "We found his horse, Señor. But we did not find him."

Total silence filled the night for one horrible, stunned moment. Then Stuart, cursing beneath his breath, turned for the door. "We're going back," he yelled, his voice breaking. "We're going back to look for him."

Deborah clutched the windowsill as the room began to spin. "No," she cried softly. "*No!*"

Below her, she could hear footsteps racing over the floors; doors slammed, men yelled. It took enormous self-restraint for Deborah not to go downstairs and offer . . . something. But she felt her presence was unwelcome in this kind of crisis. There was nothing she could do for Ridge—except pray.

She dropped to her knees beside the bed, her eyes spilling tears down her cheek, her throat too tight to speak.

She struggled, trying to find the right words, trying to call forth an urgent desperate prayer that would save Ridge's life . . . if he were still alive.

CHAPTER 8

DEBORAH'S TERROR AND GRIEF were soon lifted, though it seemed like hours had passed. Loud shouts drew her from the room and out to the hallway. All the bedroom doors were flung wide, all except Torie's. Deborah wondered how the child could possibly remain asleep in this kind of hysteria.

Clutching her wrapper tightly about her, Deborah inched her way down the hall. The sconces overhead cast light into the shadowed places as she moved toward the stairway, then hesitated.

She strained her ears to hear what the loud voices were saying, but the sounds were coming from the back yard. Lifting her trailing skirt, she crept barefooted down the winding stairway.

At the foot of the stairs, she crept toward the kitchen, seeking Margarita, but she had apparently joined the crowd outside. Deborah crept toward the open door, her heart racing.

Stuart and Adell were throwing their arms about

Ridge! Juan and Ignacio were examining a man, bound and gagged and slung over a slab-ribbed horse. Ridge had captured the thief, after all!

Deborah suppressed a cry of joy as her eyes flew back to Ridge. In the graying light of dawn, she could see that his clothes were rumpled, his face haggard; his hair, missing the usual hat, was windblown and tousled. But a look of triumph lit the dark eyes and a wide smile creased his face.

Deborah took a deep breath, forcing her taut muscles to slowly relax at the welcome sight of Ridge. She hugged her arms against her, trying to restrain herself from bursting outside to join the happy reunion. She could not, of course. Her joy faded at the sight of Adell's tall, robed figure.

But at least he was safe, she told herself, turning to creep back up the darkened stairway to her room.

Later in the morning, Deborah could smell coffee brewing and went down to the kitchen. To her surprise, Ridge sat alone at the oval table in the kitchen.

Her heart lurched at the sight of him. He was staring intently into his cup, his face bearing the shadow of a beard, his rumpled clothing testimony to his dangerous mission. She bit her lip, wondering if she should turn and slip back up the stairs. It would be easier that way. But the joy that filled her at seeing him kept her from retreating.

"Good morning," she said from the doorway.

Slowly he lifted weary eyes to her. She watched the expression change to one of surprise, then happiness as he stared at her.

"Good morning," he grinned.

Their gazes locked, and for a moment neither spoke. Then Deborah forced herself to break free of those captivating dark eyes and she hurried around to the stove to life the huge coffee pot from the burner.

"What happened last night?" she asked, pouring the steaming liquid into a small cup.

"We caught the leader of the gang who's been rustling our cattle," he said. "The rest got away, unfortunately. They're probably headed into Mexico by now. But I believe the cattle rustling is over for a while."

"I'm glad," she murmured, glancing at him over the rim of her cup.

"I missed you," he said softly.

Deborah caught her breath. The trauma of the night had made her forget, for a while, her resolution to stay away from him. But she remembered Adell's words and the old pain settled around her heart once more. She lifted her chin bravely and forced her words to sound polite, yet remote.

"Thank you. I've been quite busy. Well, good day."

"Where are you going?" he said, pulling himself out of the chair.

"Good morning, dear!" Adell's voice rang through the kitchen.

"Good morning, Mother," Ridge replied, never taking his eyes from Deborah as she turned and hurried back up the stairs.

Deborah found herself torn with conflicting emotions. Each time she was near Ridge, she had to fight her feelings and constantly remind herself of what Adell had said. At the same time, her instincts told her Ridge had been honest with her. Yet, how could she discover the truth without asking him, outright? And the very thought of doing that made her flush with embarrassment.

Her heart was not in her work, and by lunch time, she welcomed an opportunity to stroll down to the kitchen to chat with Margarita, who always had a cheering effect on her.

The person she encountered in the kitchen was not Margarita, however; it was Ridge. He was prowling through the cabinets, eager for a lunch not yet prepared. At the sight of him, she turned to leave, but he caught up with her in the hallway.

"Deborah?"

She turned, forcing a polite smile.

"Could I speak with you for a minute?"

"I'm really very busy," she responded quickly, gathering her skirts to ascend the stairs.

A hand grasped her elbow, slowly turning her back around. Her shocked eyes dropped to the hand, then traveled slowly to the dark, brooding face.

"Surely you can spare a few minutes. If you're too busy for conversation, then you're obviously over-worked. I'll speak to Mother—"

"No!" Deborah interrupted, gently pulling her arm free of his grip. "What did you want to discuss?"

A frown rumpled the dark brow as he grasped her elbow again.

"This way please," he said, gently pulling her toward the back door.

She thought of protesting again, but finally decided perhaps the easiest way to handle the situation was to relent to his request to talk. Then she would make her excuses and escape again. While she followed him silently, her arm grew rigid beneath his touch. When he glanced at her, he could see a flash of anger in her green eyes.

To Deborah's relief the back veranda was deserted. As she took her seat on the edge of a wooden chair and glanced anxiously about, she wondered what Adell would think if she caught her talking with Ridge again. Deborah took a deep breath, too frustrated by Ridge's persistence to wonder how she would respond to Adell if she were lurking in the background.

"After spending the night chasing outlaws, I'm in no mood to be brushed off, Deborah." He stood over her, watching her carefully. "I want to know why you're avoiding me."

Her eyes dropped beneath his piercing stare. She studied her needle-pricked fingers, clutched tightly in her lap. Did he really care what she felt, she wondered, as the old hurt slipped back into her heart.

"Since you were not, shall we say, cool and evasive before I left for San Francisco, I had to deduce that something happened while I was away to change your attitude. What was it?"

The dark eyes were boring through her, demanding an answer.

"Was it mother?" he pressed.

Deborah swallowed, glancing up at him. "Why should I be upset with your mother?" she managed to respond.

His face was grimly determined as he leaned down to look her squarely in the eye. "Was it my mother?"

She looked away, unable to face him now. What should she do? It would only cause more problems if she made Ridge angry with Adell, and yet—didn't he deserve her honesty?

For a long moment she stared down into the valley,

watching the veil of mist drape the orange groves like a curtain of gauze.

"What did she say?" The voice was low and soothing, and with the gentle voice came a hand on hers, tenderly clasping her fingers.

Deborah whirled back to him, her eyes filled with pain.

"I didn't know you were going into politics," she said, her voice a mere whisper. "And I've begun to feel that, well," she looked away, slipping her hand from him, "that you may be merely toying with my emotions."

A tense silence hung between them. Deborah's eyes froze on a bent sycamore as she sat rigid, awaiting his reply. For one second she sensed that he was not going to deny her fears. Then slowly he got to his feet, his hand thrust to the back of his neck as he paced back and forth across the veranda. Finally, he came back to her side and tilted his head to study her curiously.

"Deborah, I have not been toying with your emotions," he slowly answered. "Do you honestly think I would do that?"

She saw hurt in his dark eyes.

"As for politics, it's been suggested by some of the local businessmen that I enter the political arena. But I think it's just that—an arena. I'm not suited for it." He turned to pace again. "I did give some thought to it because Mother and Father wanted me to, but ultimately I decided I just wouldn't be happy in politics."

Deborah swallowed, a slow blush creeping up her neck to stain her cheeks. "Then I was mistaken," she mumbled, rising to her feet.

"*Wait!*"

His hand caught her arm again.

"Don't you think you owe me an explanation? What prompted you to have these thoughts?"

Deborah glanced up into the dark face, regretting now that she had angered and insulted him. Again, she had been the victim of another of Adell's cruel schemes. The woman was heartless. Why bother to protect her now?

"Ridge," Deborah shook her head sadly, "your mother warned me that you make a habit of tampering with women's affections. Careless little flirtations, I believe she called it. And she dropped a not-so-subtle hint that your only true interest in women would be in the kind of woman who could further your political career."

Ridge stood speechless. Then he whirled around and charged for the back door.

"Ridge, wait!" she cried, aware of the damage her words could bring. "Ridge, don't say anything to her. Please!" The desperation in her tone brought him around in puzzled dismay.

"What do you mean, don't say anything to her?" he echoed, the gray eyes indignant. "She's up to her old tricks, Deborah, the same ones that drove me away before. I intend to put an end to her schemes before she goes any further."

"Ridge, wait." Her voice held a plea that brought another look of surprise to his face. "You don't understand."

"No, obviously I don't." He shook his head and sauntered back to her side. "Not only do I not understand Mother's viciousness, I don't understand why you believed her. I assumed you were a better judge of character than to take her lies as truth. I hoped you had more faith in me."

Deborah's eyes dropped shamefully to her feet. He was right! But how could she make him understand that she was vulnerable where he was concerned, that she lacked the self-confidence to believe that a man like Ridge could truly care for her.

"I know. You're right," she nodded. "I apologize."

He reached out and touched her shoulder. "My mother can be very convincing. I'm aware of that."

Slowly, Deborah lifted her eyes to his. "I should have known better. But please don't say anything to her. I can't afford to have her angry with me."

"Why?" The dark eyes swept her curiously. "You have every reason to be angry with her. I wouldn't blame you if you packed your bags and went home. You don't have to suffer through Mother's little games. You have a prolific sewing business in Los Angeles."

At his thoughtful silence, Deborah sensed that he realized he still did not know the full story. "Deborah, there's more I don't know, isn't there?" he finally asked.

"Yes." She stopped pacing and leaned against a sequoia post, staring again at the valley. "My mother accidentally spilled ink all over your mother's best dress and cloak." The answer came on a deep sigh of relief. To be able to admit the truth to him was like having a dead weight lifted from her shoulders. "We couldn't afford to pay her for the ruined garments so it was agreed that we would repay the debt with my services. Here at Cimarron for the summer."

While Deborah had tried to relate the truth in a calm

tone, she was aware of feelings of bitterness still deep within her.

"You were sacrificed," Ridge finally responded, walking over to stare down at her. "I don't understand why your mother agreed to that."

"I just told you why." Deborah took a deep breath and looked up at him. "We couldn't afford a law suit."

Ridge considered her words. "And then Mother got jealous, obviously."

Deborah nodded. "I suspect she saw you kiss me on the veranda the other night. I caught a glimpse of her entering the study when I came back inside."

"Oh." She could see the dawn of comprehension in his dark eyes as he turned to the valley.

"Ridge could we just forget this?" Deborah lifted a hand to press her throbbing forehead. "I think it would be best for everyone if we just try to go on as before."

He looked back at her, a slow grin breaking over his face. "Fine. Will you go riding with me this afternoon?"

Deborah's mouth dropped open before she pressed her lips together and stared at him in dismay. "Have you forgotten everything that's been said? I cannot ride with you, or spend any more time with you. Don't you see? It would only create more problems."

"Yes, you can," he said. "And if you don't agree, I'll confront my mother with her little scheme."

Deborah gasped, eyes widening. "That's not fair!"

"Nor is it fair for you to shut me out of your life just because of a lie. Listen to me, Deborah. I live my own life. I won't tolerate Mother's interference with my friendships. But if it will make you feel more comfortable, let me assure you that Mother won't be spying on us. She and Father are going into Los Angeles for a stockholders meeting this afternoon. We'll ride out to the Point then come back here for a cozy dinner."

"Ridge, I can't," she shook her head wearily as she turned for the back door.

"If you aren't at the stable, I'll come looking for you," he called after her.

She dashed back up the stairs to her sewing room, praying he would forget.

He did not forget. True to his word, shortly after five, a persistent knock on her door interrupted her sewing. She stared at the neat little stitches in the hem of the garment, struggling to ignore the continual knocking. Surely he would be a gentleman and go away from her door.

She found, however, that she underestimated Ridge Farrington if she thought her silence would deter him. Slowly, the door creaked open and his dark head poked around the corner. "Miss Holt," the gray eyes flashed charmingly, "you must understand that I can be quite difficult when it comes to getting my way."

She tossed the dress down and glared at him. "Yes, I'm beginning to understand that very well."

He strolled into the room, responding to her anger with a brilliant smile. "I'm waiting for you to ride with me. It's no fun to ride alone."

"I don't want to go for a ride!" she snapped. "Now please honor my decision."

He sank into the chair nearest her and crossed his arms. He was wearing dark trousers and a white linen shirt that accented his dark good looks and unnerved her completely. "On second thought, I have a much better idea. We'll go to the fiesta instead," he said.

She looked up. "What fiesta?"

"Roberto's family is celebrating the birth of twins with a fiesta tonight. I can assure you, if you've never been to a fiesta you don't know what you're missing. We won't stay long. And it'll be an experience you'll never forget."

Despite her resolve, Deborah could feel herself weakening. The idea was so appealing to her that she wavered long enough for Ridge to press his advantage.

"Say you'll go. We'll have fun; I promise."

"I don't doubt that," she said with a begrudging smile. "But I realize there was truth in your mother's words—you *are* a charmer. I sometimes feel very defenseless."

"Deborah, I'm not trying to charm you in order to deceive you," he said, his dark eyes appealingly honest. "Have you forgotten that I'm a Christian? Perhaps not as devout as you are, but nevertheless I try to live by the Bible. I'll admit to being stubborn to a fault, but I have not lied to you. Please believe me."

The straightforward manner toppled her already weakening wall of resistance, and Deborah released a heavy sigh and nodded. "You have been very kind to me, Ridge. I, in turn, have judged you, insulted you, even been hypocritical. I'm sorry," she said, a shy smile hovering on her lips.

"I forgive you," he said, standing. "Now put on your most festive gown and let's go to the celebration. I'll ask Margarita to keep an eye on Torie."

Deborah opened her mouth to suggest they invite Torie, but Ridge sensed her unspoken question and lifted a hand to protest. "We're going to the fiesta. Just us. And if there are any objections from anyone later, I will deal with them."

Deborah decided that her most festive dress was her simple gold taffeta. She hummed to herself as she hurried through her toiletries, thinking that like the cobbler's son who wore holey shoes, she lacked a party dress. But what did it matter? She was filled with a joy that she had not experienced since . . . she tried to think . . . since she and Torie had dined with Ridge in town.

She pulled the flowing skirt over her dark head and smoothed the scalloped neckline and narrow waist in place. Satisfied with her appearance, she reached for a pearl-handled brush and stroked her long, thick hair until it gleamed like dark fire. Freed from the restraining chignon, her hair swirled about her shoulders with only small clasps above her ears to restrain the thick waves.

Finally, she thrust her feet into gold satin slippers and twirled before the cheval mirror. The candlelight cast a burnished gleam over the gold taffeta that whispered softly about her slender ankles. She felt as giddy-headed as Cinderella sneaking off to the grand ball.

She stopped twirling and stared at her reflection again. Margarita's rich meals had given her a more wholesome look, while adding a couple of pounds to her slim figure. Still, the extra weight was becoming, she decided, jumping at the sound of footsteps outside her door.

A soft tapping brought her heart to her throat. She was as skittish as a colt! Casting one last inspective glance at her reflection, she turned and hurried over to open the door.

Ridge stood smiling down at her, breathtaking in his attire. He was dressed in a black suit with silver trim and looked the part of a true vaquero. The gleaming red cravat at his throat accented his dark complexion and made him more handsome than ever.

"You're beautiful." His adoring eyes swept her.

"And you're handsome!" she responded recklessly, her head tilted back to study his striking outfit.

When he reached out to pull her into his arms, she lifted a small restraining hand. "Shall we go?" she asked, her tone mildly reproving.

A reluctant grin tugged at his lips as his eyes darted over her again. "If we must," he sighed.

"Where's Torie?" Deborah asked as they hurried down the hall.

"I bribed Margarita," he whispered, placing his hand on her elbow to guide her down the stairs. "She's in Torie's room learning the fine art of checker playing."

Deborah lifted a hand to her mouth to smother a giggle, as they turned up the hall and stepped onto the veranda, illuminated tonight by hazed gas lamps.

"My carriage awaits," he said, brandishing his arm in a grand gesture toward the buckboard, hitched to a pair of gleaming bays.

"And a fine one it is," she lifted her skirts, smiling up at him.

"My parents took the carriage into town," he said, more seriously, "and I didn't relish the idea of going in the brougham with a driver to spoil our privacy. I hope you don't mind." His grin was apologetic, almost shy—which was a rare expression on the face of Ridge Farrington, Deborah thought, with amusement.

"Good idea," she nodded her approval as he assisted her up into the seat.

"We haven't far to go," he promised, dashing around to hoist himself up on the driver's side.

He clicked the reins over the horses, whose coats gleamed like brown satin in the darkness. Deborah's admiring gaze moved from the horses to the shadowed yard and finally the brawny outstretched arms of the leafy oaks.

She sighed. The night was drowned in soft darkness and filled with the fragrance of a thousand roses. She could feel contentment slipping over her, and again she sighed.

"Talk to me, Deborah," Ridge looked across at her. "I want to know everything about you."

Slowly, she turned her head to arch a teasing brow. "Everything? What if I don't wish to tell you everything?"

"Then I'll just have to devise some plan to coax out your deepest, darkest secrets!"

Deborah laughed. "Let's see," she tilted her head back and studied a distant star. "First, you should know that I'm an only child. And I suppose my parents must have lived in fear that I would grow into a spoiled little brat, because they raised half the neighborhood. I can't remember a time when our store wasn't crowded with children, sucking on peppermint sticks or dawdling over toys." She sighed, remembering. "Our meager table was always crowded with church families, or cousins, or someone who had drifted into the store at closing time and decided to stay for supper."

Her voice trailed away as she glanced at Ridge. The dark eyes watched her with growing fascination.

"Most of our fellowships we shared with church families. We had a very strong bond with the families from our little church."

Ridge nodded, guiding the horses into a narrow adobe street filled with small, flower-vined cabins. Candles winked from every window in the little settlement, and the rhythmical flow of conversations in Spanish reached their ears.

"This is Roberto's neighborhood," Ridge smiled. "Of course he lives at Cimarron now, but all of his family is still here. He once told me he had fifteen cousins."

As they approached the first cabin, a door flew open and Roberto ran out to meet them.

At the sound of his voice, other doors were flung wide, and suddenly the narrow street was filled with people.

As Deborah watched the crowd grow, she realized that the street was the only logical place for a gathering of so many.

Ridge hopped down from the buckboard then came around to assist Deborah. Since her Spanish was limited, she could scarcely follow the many phrases that were lovingly spoken, but she extended her hand and offered a wide smile to all.

Ridge, on the contrary, fell into rapid Spanish, conversing easily with some of the older men. The women were dressed in ruffled, lace-trimmed dresses that complemented their gleaming dark hair and eyes. All of the men, like Ridge, wore the black suits common to the vaquero.

As Deborah stood glancing around, she was conscious suddenly of the rhythmical movement somewhere in the distance. The ground beneath her began to quiver with the staccato stomping of slippers and boots as castanets began to click and several guitars strummed a throbbing rhythm. As the music swelled, the crowd spread into a large circle. The younger couples entered the center of the circle and began to participate in native dances, while the older people clapped their hands and shouted encouragement.

Ridge's arm slipped protectively around her shoulder as he grinned at her upturned face. Deborah found herself nestling into the curve of his arm, aware that she could become spoiled to that protective feeling.

A persistent tug at her skirt brought her glance downward to a small boy who stood, head tilted back to appraise her for a moment, before pointing behind her. She turned to see what he was trying to tell her and spotted a plump, older woman stringing a papier-mâché donkey to the rafter of a low-roofed adobe nearby.

"Look." Deborah nudged Ridge. "I've always wanted to watch this game."

A red bandana served as a blindfold to the little boy who had tugged Deborah's skirt. The children were crowding around now, jumping with excitement and elbowing each other gleefully as the woman placed a long stick in the boy's hand.

The little boy lunged forward, widely brandishing the stick in search of the gaily-decorated piñata. Deborah and Ridge watched, exchanging amused glances, as he narrowly missed and the children shouted encouragement to the boy. Again, he struck out and missed, but cocking his ear to one side he caught the whir of the swinging rope and this time he leaped forward and struck the edge of the piñata. Candy and trinkets spiraled through the air, landing in eager, outstretched hands.

Behind them the music swelled, along with laughter and the melodious hum of a few voices, joining in a

Spanish love song. Deborah watched affectionately, thrilled by the sight of so many happy people. But again someone was tugging at her sleeve, pulling her vision from the joyous crowd.

A dark-eyed woman was motioning them inside her humble yet immaculate adobe where a long table of food was placed near the door.

Ridge began to offer praises in Spanish as he spied the food. Then, remembering Deborah's confusion, he turned back. "This is Roberto's mother," he explained.

In the center of the table, candles gleamed in silver candelabra surrounded by rose petals floating in small dishes of water.

Impulsively, Ridge reached forward to pluck a rose petal from the water, then drying it on his sleeve, he gently inserted it beneath the clasp in Deborah's hair, just above her ear.

"Si," Roberto's mother nodded eagerly, her eyes glowing with admiration as she stared wide-eyed at Deborah.

Deborah was unaware of the lovely vision she presented, with the scarlet rose in her hair, accenting her creamy skin and flashing green eyes.

Ridge, however, stood staring at her, unable to break the magic that bound them together as Deborah returned his steady gaze. The soft laughter of the woman shook them back to their senses, and they turned to survey, with astonishment, the enormous array of food.

There were fresh, meat-stuffed tortillas, green tamales, olive-topped enchiladas, a variety of vegetables, beans and rice, and for desert, fudge cakes and fruit pies.

At the woman's steady persistence, Ridge and Deborah filled tin plates with food and wandered onto the doorstep to eat as they watched the party in the street. The little woman kept urging more food on them until finally Deborah pressed a hand to her stomach and emphatically shook her head.

"Ridge, please tell her I enjoyed her meal, but if I eat anything more, I'll be sick all the way home."

Ridge chuckled and relayed the message to the pleased little woman who nodded with a smile.

Deborah's lashes grew heavy as the music slowed to a soothing lullaby and Ridge, catching her sleepy gaze, made their excuses and they bid the crowd a pleasant good evening.

Later, as they rode home, the steady clomping of the horse hooves on the dark road was the only sound in the velvet night. Deborah found herself giving in to Ridge's tugging arm and nestling her sleepy head against his shoulder.

When finally the buckboard drew up before the front door, and Ridge escorted her up the veranda, she turned to voice her thanks for a perfect evening.

She soon realized that Ridge expected more than a mere thank you. He gathered her into his arms and leaned down to inhale the sweet fragrance of the rose, still tucked in dark strands of hair.

"Mmmm," he sniffed, then tilted her chin back to look deep into her emerald eyes. "Paradise," he whispered.

His lips dipped to brush hers and that odd tingling that he always inspired jangled through her. Suddenly she was wide awake! As his arms encircled her, she pulled away, afraid and shy. He sensed her reluctance and leaned down to look at her.

"I'm so glad you came to Cimarron, Deborah," he said. "I'm sorry about the unhappy circumstances but I'm beginning to see the wisdom of God's plan."

She considered his words, wondering if their relationship could possibly be a part of God's plan for her life. Was it too much to long to be loved by a man like Ridge? Could he possibly love her? Hope spiraled through her, making her dizzy with anticipation.

The romance of the evening had cast its magic upon both of them, and Deborah was in no mood to rationalize when it was so much easier to hope . . . to dream. . . .

This time when Ridge leaned forward to kiss her, she wound her arms around his neck and let him hold her tightly.

CHAPTER 9

THE JOY OF THE PREVIOUS EVENING was shattered the next afternoon when Adell returned. With Ridge gone for the day, and Torie reading the Bible in her room, Deborah had been free to work on her sewing, catching up on the work she had missed. Just when Deborah had convinced herself there might be a real purpose in her coming to Cimarron, her hopes were destroyed by Adell's abrupt entrance into her room.

"How dare you!" she shouted, her cheeks flushed, her blue eyes leaping with rage.

"I . . . beg your pardon?" Deborah stammered, the blouse she was mending slipping from her hands.

The big woman marched over to her and stood with her hands clenched in fists in the folds of her silk dress. "You know very well I have forbidden anyone instilling religion in Torie. Yet you dared give her your Bible and insist that she read it."

"I—"

"Spare me your excuses! You have also defied my

wishes and carried on with my son! Torie told me the two of you slipped off someplace last evening and didn't return until late.''

At those words, Deborah's eyes dropped guiltily to her lap. Both of her accusations were true, but how could she make the woman understand that she meant no harm?

"You'll not get another opportunity to flaunt yourself or your silly religion in my house!" she shrieked furiously. "Finish every one of these dresses as quickly as possible, then get out of my house. When your trunk is packed, inform Juan and he'll drive you to town.''

She whirled on her heel and swept from the room, slamming the door. Deborah slumped into the chair, staring blankly into space, as the brisk steps charged back down the hall.

Her dark lashes blinked rapidly, as she struggled to keep her composure. She *had* defied Adell's wishes; how could she argue with that? But why had Torie told her mother? And why had she made an innocent evening with Ridge sound wicked?

Deborah's lashes drooped at the memory of his kiss, and that ecstatic moment in his arms. Maybe the evening hadn't been so innocent after all.

Suddenly, a rush of defensive anger filled her and she jumped to her feet. It didn't matter if she encountered Adell again, she decided, opening her door and hurrying down the hall to Torie's room. She had to talk to Torie.

She knocked softly on Torie's door, and at the muffled response, she twisted the knob and entered.

Torie's bedroom was decorated in rich lemon and white trim, but the cheerful decor was lost on

Deborah today. She sucked in a deep breath as her eyes scanned the luxurious room, seeking Torie.

She found her, crumpled in a heap in the center of her small bed.

The girl sat up on her elbow, her eyes red, her face streaked with tears. And on her right cheek was the glaring red imprint of a large hand.

All of Deborah's anger suddenly fled at the sight of the ugly print on the delicate little face.

"Oh, Torie," she sighed, closing the door and hurrying across to her side. Without saying more, she sat on the edge of the bed and gathered the weeping girl into her arms, hugging her tightly against her.

"She . . . slapped me," Torie sobbed, pushing back to look into Deborah's face. "She came in and caught me reading your Bible. And she hit me hard."

Tears poured from her wounded eyes, coursing down the thin cheeks, angling across the crimson handprint.

"I know," Deborah whispered. "I'm so sorry."

Torie buried her face in Deborah's neck, her tiny shoulders heaving in wrenching sobs. Deborah pulled her tighter against her, trying to absorb some of the heartbreak, hoping to press some of her own strength into the frail little body. As she sat holding the girl, letting her pour out her anger and heartache, Deborah's eyes roamed absently over the room then jerked to a halt.

Tossed in the center of the floor was her Bible, pages torn, cover dangling. Suddenly, she felt like weeping, too. Adell had reacted with a harshness that was far from normal.

The little fingers were pressing into her shoulders as Torie pushed back from her and flopped into her pillows. The hurt that had filled the blue irises moments before was changing now, replaced by something stronger—a bitterness that twisted her features and stopped her flow of tears.

"It's all your fault!" she lashed out. "Why did you have to come here talking about your God? Telling me to read your Bible! Now, look where it got me. I can't even leave my room!"

Deborah felt as though an invisible hand had just smashed her cheek. Though there was no handprint to bear evidence of the blow, the hurt vibrated through her, touching every fiber of her being.

Her eyes bore the glazed look of one in mild shock. Her mouth was too dry to speak. She could only gape at the child whose hurt and anger had found an easy target.

"I told Mother about you and Ridge, too." Her lips twisted in grim satisfaction. "She says the only reason you're being so nice to me is just so you can get Ridge. You're just like the others back in Santa Fe," her lips curled bitterly. "No, you're even worse. They never pretended to be goodie-goodies like you. I believed you were different," she cried, "but you're not. And I hate you. *I hate you!* I'll be glad when you're gone."

The high wail became a shriek of agony, one that drove Deborah from the room dumb with shock. She stumbled blindly down the hall to her room. With trembling fingers, she locked the doors, shutting out a household that had suddenly gone mad.

Like one possessed, Deborah worked through the night, ignoring the soft tapping on her door, refusing Margarita's offers of food. She had made her mind up to see no one, particularly Ridge, until her work was

123

finished and she could flee from Cimarron. Then she would gladly leave the Farringtons and all the pain they had caused her. She felt another stab of pain when she thought of saying goodbye to Ridge, but she had no choice. What chance did they possibly have when his mother and sister hated her?

At dawn, she fell over her work table, too exhausted to drag herself to bed. She did not hear the key turning in the lock nor the soft footsteps that crossed the carpet to her side.

A shocked Ridge stared down at her pale face, the mussed hair, the needle-pricked fingers. Gently, he lifted her from the chair and swung her into his arms. Her head toppled back onto his shoulder, but she was too exhausted to realize she was being moved. Ever so gently, he lowered her onto her bed then pulled up the quilt. He took a deep quivering breath as he stood staring down at the delicate features relaxed now in sleep.

As he stared, a warning began to tick in the back of his mind. The smoky gray eyes turned as hard as the metal on his gun barrel as he turned and charged from the room.

Dawn was just breaking over the horizon, although he was already dressed for work. His boots made steady thuds along the Brussels carpet as he drew up before his mother's door and hammered impatiently.

"I demand to know what you're up to," he said, when finally his mother opened the door.

She belted her satin robe and lifted a hand to push her silver hair from sleepy eyes.

"Ridge, have you been drinking?" She fixed accusing eyes on his grim face. "It isn't even morning."

"It's morning for me," he barked. "I'm an early

riser, in case you've forgotten. Only *this* morning, I came upstairs to check on a strange report from Margarita, that Deborah had locked herself in her room and refused food. I came up and discovered a faint light seeping from beneath her door. When I got a key and entered, I found her crumpled over the sewing table. As I suspected, she is ill—probably worked herself into exhaustion. What are you up to, Mother?'' The dark eyes narrowed dangerously as he glared at Adell.

''Me?'' Adell lifted a hand to her bosom, indignant. ''Why do you have to leap to the conclusion that I'm to blame? If the lazy girl can't keep up with her work, I hardly see how I'm to blame.''

''What's going on?'' Stuart Farrington thundered across the room.

''Miss Holt has either been locked in her room or has been subjected to some form of cruelty that has caused her to seek seclusion.''

Stuart turned to his wife, an angry white line circling his thin lips. ''Can you explain this?''

The woman glanced from one man to another. Apparently sensing she was outnumbered, she chose the tack of humility.

''Why, I had nothing to do with Miss Holt working herself into exhaustion. Surely you know I have better sense than to make unreasonable demands now. The Warrens are coming soon—or have you forgotten?'' She glanced at Stuart, an unspoken threat in her tone.

Both men considered her reasoning, exchanging glances. What she was saying made sense to them, knowing Adell would never deprive herself of extra help when guests were arriving.

''Mother, I still believe there's something going on

that I don't know about." Ridge stood glaring at her. "So let me remind you of something: I came home again after you promised not to interfere in my life. You've already done that by suggesting to Deborah that I am no more than a heartbreaker and a social climber."

He waved aside Adell's protest. "The only reason I haven't confronted you about this sooner was because Deborah pleaded with me not to. But," he lowered his face to hers, the dark eyes challenging her, "if you do anything like that again, I'll leave. And this time I won't come back. Not ever."

He turned and strode down the hall, leaving Adell to stare speechlessly after him. His words brought a sudden pallor to her skin as Stuart glowered at her.

She wrung her hands together.

"Stuart, dear," she turned back to her husband with a pleading smile, "I am so dreadfully sorry. You must help me calm Ridge down."

CHAPTER 10

WHEN DEBORAH AWOKE, the morning sun was already streaming across her room. She sat up abruptly, rubbing her sore eyes, glancing dazedly about her. She didn't remember going to her bed. All she remembered was the backbreaking night she had spent, driving herself mercilessly in order to complete her sewing.

She lifted her hand and stared down at the pricked skin on her fingers. Her vision had blurred toward morning, and she had jabbed herself with the needle numerous times.

A heavy sigh shook her small frame as she recalled the horrid events of the night before. Foremost in her mind now, was Torie. The hateful words Torie had spoken had pierced Deborah's heart, hurting as nothing ever had. But now, in the cold light of morning, she realized she had to speak to Torie again.

She dragged herself off the bed and stumbled to her wash basin. Empty. She recalled Margarita's persistent knocks the night before, but Deborah had ignored her. She hadn't wanted to see or talk with anyone. She sighed, peering drearily into the cheval mirror at her swollen eyes and mussed hair. Yawning, she lifted the pearl-handled brush and dragged it through the tangled strands of her hair, then subdued it with a ribbon. Her feet were like lead as she dragged herself to the wardrobe and pulled out a simple, dark cotton dress. All the while her thoughts lingered on Torie.

She had to assure her that she never intended to cause problems. That she would never, ever use Torie to get to Ridge. Obviously, others had done this, and the unfairness of that was still fresh in the girl's mind.

Her thoughts flowed more coherently as her fingers flew over the bodice of her dress, smoothing out wrinkles. Tossing one last glance at her reflection in the mirror, she opened the door and marched resolutely down the hall to Torie's room.

She hesitated, wondering if Torie were awake. Then she quickly decided it didn't matter. She could not prolong this conversation. With new resolve, she lifted her hand and tapped softly on the door. A weak voice invited her in.

Slowly, Deborah turned the knob and peered around the corner of the door. Torie was dressed and seated at her desk, attempting to patch Deborah's torn Bible.

The sight brought a rush of tenderness to Deborah's heart, and she quietly crossed the room to stand beside Torie. "You don't have to do that," she said, watching the child's awkward attempts to rebind the pages.

"Yes, I do," she swallowed, her small fingers fumbling with the torn pages. "It needs mending—

like me!'' Slowly she lifted her face to Deborah and tears spilled from her eyes. ''I guess it takes your God to mend a person inside,'' she sniffed.

''Yes, it does,'' Deborah whispered, laying a comforting hand on Torie's thin shoulder. After Adell's threats and punishment, Deborah could not scold Torie for her cruel behavior the night before. Torie had obviously learned an important truth, and for that Deborah was grateful.

Slowly, almost reverently, Torie laid the Bible down and turned to Deborah. Shyly, she laid her head on Deborah's shoulder as she began to sob. ''I didn't mean what I said, Deborah. You're the best friend I ever had. Will you forgive me?''

''Of course I will,'' Deborah's lips were trembling as she hugged the heaving body against her.

''Good morning.'' Adell stood in the open door, observing the emotional scene impassively.

Deborah's spine stiffened, as she turned to face her. This time she would defend the child and herself, regardless of the consequences. Adell's bullying was over.

To her dismay, however, the woman's tone was strangely humble when she spoke. ''I must ask both of you to forgive me,'' she said quietly. ''I was not myself yesterday.'' Her jeweled hands were clasped tightly before her. ''I had been suffering from one of my migraine headaches. Otherwise, I would not have behaved so badly.''

Torie and Deborah stared at her, unable to reply. Suddenly Adell's eyes dropped to the torn Bible on Torie's dresser. ''I'll replace your Bible, Deborah,'' she mumbled stiffly.

''That isn't necessary. I can repair it myself,'' Deborah answered, her tone reserved.

"You did willfully go against my wishes," she reminded her. At those words, Torie slipped out of Deborah's arms and sauntered over to flounce onto her bed. "You knew I wanted Torie to wait until she was older to make her own decision concerning a religion. But I'm willing to overlook that," a spark of kindness touched her blue eyes, "if both of you will forgive my behavior yesterday."

Deborah glanced at Torie who was drawing imaginary circles on her bedspread with a slim little finger. "I forgive you," Deborah replied, knowing she had to bridge the gap.

The older woman turned to Torie, the blue eyes sweeping over the indifferent child. "Torie, I intend to make up to you for . . . what I did." She cleared her throat. "We'll take a nice little trip after the Warrens leave. Perhaps I'll take you with me on my next trip to San Francisco? Would you like that?" she asked, speaking in a hurried, breathless tone.

Torie's thin shoulders lifted in a careless shrug, but the blue eyes widened curiously as she turned to look at her mother.

"And Deborah," Adell pushed a stiff smile on to her lips, "please do not leave Cimarron. Not yet. Unless you want to, of course," she quickly added, studying Deborah's guarded expression. "Take the day off—go into Los Angeles if you wish. Juan isn't busy today. I could ask him to hitch up the carriage and drive you in."

Deborah was already shaking her head. She had no desire to visit her mother today. There would be no way she could conceal her heartache, and her mother didn't need more problems.

"I'm too tired for a trip to town," she responded,

"but thank you anyway." She glanced at Torie, whose sad eyes made silent pleas to her. "Perhaps Torie and I will relax together."

"Whatever you wish," a hint of jealousy crept into Adell's tone but she forced herself to remain polite. "And now if I've made my peace, shall we all have breakfast?"

Deborah tried to appear pleasant at the breakfast table, despite the subtle undercurrent of tension present. For a change, the entire family was dining together and this struck Deborah as odd.

Stuart Farrington, seated at the end of the table, seemed mysteriously tense. Why had he delayed his morning trip to town, Deborah wondered, glancing across at Torie. Did he know about his wife's cruel display of temper?

Torie's smooth, pale cheek bore no evidence of her mother's handprint, and Deborah doubted that Torie would volunteer the information, having been intimidated by Adell. She sighed, saddened by the tragic events.

"I have some exciting plans," Adell announced brightly. She was dressed in blazing red silk and her face, at this early hour, was heavily rouged. "I've decided to follow your suggestions about clearing a patch of land for tennis, Ridge. Torie does need a sport she can enjoy." The blue eyes lingered on her daughter's surprised face, as Adell gave her a placating smile. "Would you like that, Torie?"

"Oh, yes!" Torie perked up. "When could we start playing?"

"Very soon, dear," her mother's thin mouth spread in a patronizing smile.

Deborah glanced across the table to Ridge, awaiting

his reaction. To her surprise, he made no comment, but merely picked at his food. Her eyes returned to her plate, a blank expression crossing her face. It was impossible to understand the Farringtons. Each was so unpredictable.

"What are your plans for the day, Deborah?" Ridge suddenly asked, startling her from her wandering thoughts.

She looked across at Torie, remembering her promise. "Torie and I are going to make some plans—maybe go on a picnic?" Her voice lifted in an effort to instill some enthusiasm in herself, as well as Torie.

"Oh, yes," Torie said. "I'd love to go on a picnic."

"I'll be ready in a few minutes," Deborah replied, rising from her chair. She murmured her appreciation to Margarita for the meal, then turned to leave the room.

"Deborah," Ridge reached her at the door, "you look tired," he said, his eyes sweeping her with concern.

Deborah's eyes drifted back to Adell, who was quietly studying her coffee cup.

"I'm fine," she murmured, aware that Stuart Farrington was watching her as well.

"Excuse us, Torie," Ridge said as his sister hovered near Deborah. With a disgusted sigh, she wandered off. Ridge took Deborah's arm and led her out of the room.

"What are you doing?" she asked, as he suddenly took her arm and propelled her up the hall.

"I want to talk to you privately," he said, pushing the front door open.

Deborah resisted the impulse to pull her arm loose

132

as the cool morning air rushed over her, fanning her warm cheeks. She glanced again at Ridge who was staring down at her with a mixture of curiosity and concern. "How could you be fine when you worked through the night, Deborah?" he asked softly.

She blinked in surprise, then turned to stare across the veranda. She crossed her arms, searching her mind for the right words. Finally, she decided the only way to respond to his question was to avoid the main issue.

"Ridge, your friendship has meant a great deal to me," she finally replied. "But I'm afraid it only complicates my life right now."

A frown knitted his dark brows together. "Why?"

"Because I came here to work for your mother, and I must get along with her. I can take care of myself and," she swallowed, "and I don't need you to defend me. So stop worrying," she added gently.

He released her arm and leaned against the door frame. "Perhaps I don't know you as well as I thought. Are you trying to play the role of martyr?" he asked, anger flaring in his dark eyes.

"No, of course not," she said, her frayed nerves sharpening her tone. "There was an argument," she admitted, "but your mother apologized. Nothing else matters now. Ridge," she touched his hand, "please let me work out my problems alone."

She turned and hurried inside, trying to erase from her mind the wounded look in his eyes. *How could she please everyone?* she wondered frantically, as she slowly walked up the stairs.

She couldn't please everyone, she finally admitted to herself. For now Ridge would just have to respect her wishes and try to understand. If she told him everything that had happened, he would confront Adell and there would be more trouble. The important thing was to smooth over the last crisis, then attempt to forget it.

She entered her room and closed the door, her back pressed against it as she thought of Torie. The poor girl needed her friendship and Ridge would only interfere.

Ridge . . .

Her heart ached as she thought of their hopeless romance. She was falling in love with him. She had never in her life fought so hard against a relationship and still, it had happened. She trudged wearily across the room, her sleeplessness taking its toll on her lifeless body.

Suddenly, the door was flung open and Torie flew into the room, a calico bonnet on her head, a basket swinging from her hand.

"Ready to go on our picnic?" Torie asked, her blue eyes bright with anticipation.

"Yes. Why not?" Deborah forced a pleasant smile.

The next day Deborah awakened with new enthusiasm. The temperature had dropped during the night, and the fresh air drifting through the window was cool and invigorating. She dressed quickly, choosing a soft blue muslin gown with long fitted sleeves, then she tiptoed down the hall, aware by the surrounding silence that most of the household was still sleeping. Saturday mornings were a time of relaxing from the busy week. Margarita also seemed to be moving at a more relaxed pace as Deborah entered the kitchen.

"Good morning, Margarita."

"Good morning, Señorita," Margarita nodded, the

glowing eyes sweeping Deborah quickly before she hurried to pour her a cup of coffee.

"What a lovely morning it is," Deborah glanced toward the open door. Golden sunshine beckoned and on an impulse Deborah took her coffee and walked out to the veranda to enjoy the fresh air. Her steps came to an abrupt halt in the doorway, however, as she caught sight of Ridge, seated at a table, a brooding frown rumpling his forehead.

He was dressed in work clothes, yet his dark hair was neatly combed and his face freshly shaven. A suntanned hand cradled a cup of coffee, untouched. He appeared to be lost in his thoughts. What was he thinking, she wondered, her eyes flicking cautiously over him before she quietly turned to slip back inside, but he heard her steps.

"Deborah." He uncoiled his long frame and stood. "Come join me." There was a sudden tenderness to his voice.

She hesitated, trying to think of an excuse to refuse, yet knowing it was useless to try and avoid him now. She took a deep breath and slowly walked over to stand beside him.

"How are you?" he asked, the dark eyes probing hers.

"I'm fine." Her lips tilted in a tremulous smile. "I had a good night's rest."

"You look well," he said, his eyes sweeping her with approval. She fidgeted beneath those dark, burning eyes then turned her face to the scenery before them.

"Isn't it a beautiful day," she sighed.

A gentle rain in the night and a cool breeze made everything seem fresh and new. Drops of dew clung to the rose petals, like miniature crystals.

"Yes. The weather is perfect," he agreed, turning back to the landscape that had been the source of his attention. "I was just thinking about how much I like it here. I wish things could be different."

She opened her mouth then pressed her lips together, carefully choosing her words. "God has a plan for each of us," she finally replied. "My father used to remind me of that so many times." She lifted her chin and tried to draw strength from her own words. "I suppose it takes time to discover that plan," she added softly.

"Sometimes the waiting is difficult," Ridge shook his dark head and heaved a sigh. "It's amusing the way Mother and Torie keep referring to the women in my life, Deborah. You must think I've been quite a ladies' man. The truth is, I've had many friends, but I've never been serious about a woman—until you."

He reached for her hand. She felt the strength in his fingers ebbing into her own as her gaze was drawn to his. "Deborah, I've only known you a short time, but I believe a man can know, almost instinctively, when the right woman comes along. *I* know. I'm falling in love with you."

Deborah felt her mouth dropping open as his words registered. Her heart raced in her chest as she stared, wide-eyed, into the lean, handsome face above her. *Could it really be true?* Did Ridge love her the way she loved him? She wanted desperately to believe that, but somehow she couldn't.

"I realize this may come as a shock to you," he was saying, "but I had to tell you how I feel. Maybe you don't feel the same way. . . ."

She blinked, dazed. Could he possibly doubt her love? On the other hand, was she ready to admit it?

Was she *sure?* Shyness warred with fear as a tentative smile crossed her lips.

"Ridge," she reached for his hand, "I—"

"Good morning." Stuart Farrington stood in the back door, a smile on his thin face. Then his eyes fell to their clasped hands and he quickly looked away, an amused grin tugging at his mouth.

Deborah withdrew her hand, her cheeks flaming. No doubt, Stuart Farrington had overhead most of their conversation! Her eyes flew over him, searching for his reaction and saw a look of pleasure light his face as he glanced back at them.

"Good morning," Ridge placed his cup on the table and turned to his father.

"I've let my coffee get cold," Deborah said, lifting her untouched coffee cup. "Please excuse me."

"I'll see you later," Ridge called as she hurriedly crossed the veranda, offering a shy smile to Stuart.

"Have a pleasant morning," Stuart smiled back.

Deborah sailed back up the stairs on wings of love. She could hardly believe that Ridge was in love with her. Or that Stuart Farrington seemed to silently offer his blessings. Still, this was happening despite Adell's interference. Sue paused on the second floor, lifting a trembling hand to her chest to catch her breath. Ridge was a man of his word, she believed that, no matter what Adell had insinuated.

She plunged into her sewing with a vigor that carried her through her work in record time. When the bold knock that identified Adell sounded on her door, she fixed a bright smile on her face and cheerfully invited her in.

"You've certainly accomplished a lot," Adell's thin brows arched at the sight of the many dresses, already completed and waiting to be returned. "My, but you are efficient."

"Thank you," Deborah murmured, watching as the big woman folded her hands before her and fixed an inquisitive glance on Deborah.

"I wonder if I could ask a favor," she finally spoke, her pale lids slit as she regarded Deborah thoughtfully.

"What is it?" Deborah laid her sewing aside and looked at her curiously.

"Well, as you know, we were expecting the Warrens this week, but I've just had word they're arriving on the Southern Pacific at noon today. Naturally, we aren't ready for them," she began to nervously pace the floor. "I suppose we'll just have to make do," she said, staring through the narrow window.

"What would you like me to do?" Deborah shifted in her chair, practically holding her breath for Adell's reply.

Adell turned slowly to face her, casting a quick glance about the room. "Would it be too much of an imposition for you to move your belongings in here to the sewing room?" Adell's eyes slid away from Deborah's startled face. "I'd like Amelia to have your bedroom while they're here."

"Amelia?" Deborah echoed blankly.

"The Warrens' daughter. Surely Ridge has mentioned Amelia?" Adell's brows arched again. "Well, probably not," she waved a plump hand through the air, dismissing the matter. "Would you mind giving Amelia your bedroom?" she repeated in a tone that was more a command than a question.

Deborah dropped her eyes to the spool of thread

she was still holding, attempting to conceal the surprise she felt. "Of course not," she responded. "I can sleep on this bed, and if you and Torie want to take your dresses back to your room, there'll be plenty of room for my things in here."

"Good." A triumphant grin slit Adell's thin lips. "Well, I'd best get busy," she called over her shoulder as she swept out of the room and closed the door.

Deborah sat for a moment, staring at the closed door. Then slowly her eyes traveled over the tiny sewing room, now to be her bedroom as well.

Amelia, she repeated the name in her mind. Why did Adell think Ridge would have mentioned this Amelia?

She shook her head in confusion as she got out of the chair and hurried into the next bedroom, preparing it for the coming guest.

When the Warrens arrived, and the household was summoned to greet them, Deborah got the shock of her life. She had hurried down the stairs, anxious to meet the Farrington's lifelong friends, but one look at Amelia had struck her dumb. The tall, golden-haired girl was a vision of loveliness as she stood in the center of the hall, her exquisite blue silk gown swirling about her.

Eyes, as blue as Dresden saucers, met the elder Farringtons'. She murmured the perfect replies in a smooth cultured voice. Her alabaster skin had never suffered the sun's piercing rays, and the soft white hands were strangers to work.

Involuntarily, Deborah's own needle-pricked fingers curled against her skirt in an effort to conceal their flaws.

Amelia's parents, an attractive, gray-haired couple, were equally charming, though more subdued than Amelia who had begun to chatter about the latest political news.

Deborah cast a suspicious glance toward Adell who stood captivated by the tall blonde. With a sigh of resignation, Deborah began to inch her way backward toward the kitchen, longing to escape the embarrassing introductions. Obviously, Adell had found the perfect match for her son whose political aspirations paled in contrast to the two women chatting excitedly about women's suffrage.

"And just where is Ridge?" Amelia asked, the ruby lips feigning a pretty pout.

Stuart Farrington cleared his throat. "He was delayed in town, but I can assure you he will be along soon."

"Oh yes," Adell clasped her jeweled hands together and appraised Amelia with a conspiratory gleam. "He's looked so forward to your arrival, dear."

"Hi, Amelia," Torie dragged herself down the stairs, and fixed a bored stare on Amelia.

"Torie!" The blonde woman clasped the girl into her arms, ignoring the wince of disapproval on Torie's face.

"Have you met Deborah?" Torie asked, prying herself loose. The sound of her name froze Deborah in the kitchen door. She hesitated, only a few feet away from escape. She could feel the blood creeping to her face as all eyes riveted toward her. There was no escaping now.

"Who?" Amelia tossed her shimmering blonde hair as she looked around the room.

"Yes," Adell interjected, "come meet our seamstress, Deborah Holt. Deborah, this is Miss Amelia Warren." Deborah managed a polite greeting. There was no mistaking Adell's subtle message that she was not on their social level.

As her eyes met Adell's, the look of cold scorn chilled Deborah to the bone, but she merely lifted her chin higher, her emerald eyes unblinking. Once again, Adell had deceived her. The polite mask Adell had worn earlier was no more than that—a mask to convince everyone she was capable of tenderness, even humility. But nothing had changed.

"Your own seamstress in residence?" the sedate Mrs. Warren queried.

"She's more than a seamstress," Stuart Farrington spoke up as he walked over to stand beside Deborah. "She's become a dear friend as well."

Deborah glanced at the man who had once seemed so formidable. As his dark eyes slipped back to her, she smiled her appreciation. After Deborah had politely spoken to the Warrens, she turned and slipped out of the hall. Once inside the kitchen, away from the prying eyes, she made a dash for the back door.

As she stepped onto the veranda, she cast a frantic glance over her shoulder, fearing that Torie might track her down. She had to escape those prying eyes; she needed privacy in order to compose herself.

The side yard was empty now, since all the attention was centered on the guests within the house. Deborah walked slowly across the yard to a huge leafy oak where she could slip beneath the branches and hide for a while.

She swallowed against her dry mouth and lifted a hand to her breast, trying to still her pounding heart.

Breathlessly, she leaned against the gnarled trunk, willing herself to calm down and collect her thoughts. The swaying branches offered a cooling breeze and she stood very still for a moment, her dark lashes squeezed together as the sigh of the wind drifted over her. Slowly, the erratic beat of her pulse became more normal and she opened her eyes and stared dazedly across the green lawn.

There was no doubt in her mind why the Warrens had come to Cimarron! Probably everyone but Ridge was aware of the trap that was being set for him, she thought bitterly.

Distractedly, she clasped her hands together, her fingers gripped tightly. As her eyes dropped absently to her hands, she suddenly recalled how Ridge had held her hands earlier, how he had declared his love for her.

The memory of that special moment strengthened her now. Poor Ridge, she sighed, recalling the determined gleam in Adell's and Amelia's eyes.

The sound of hoofbeats on the graveled drive below drew her attention. She peered around the gnarled trunk of the tree and a gasp rose in her throat at the sight of Ridge thundering up to the house.

The sight of him also brought an ache to her heart. She loved him so much, but her instincts warned her that she was in great danger of losing him now. She didn't doubt that he loved her, she believed him; but if he also had strong feelings for the beautiful Amelia, Deborah feared she would soon pale in comparison.

She flattened herself against the trunk of the tree at the sound of the sweet voice ringing from the veranda, calling his name. He yanked the black stallion to a halt at the hitching rail, then bounded off, jerking his felt hat from his head. The bright sunlight flooded his face, exposing for all to see the sudden look of joy that touched his features.

Deborah gripped a branch, her senses already warning her that she was about to be hurt, that she should turn back to the house rather than spy on the couple. But it was too late to retreat, and she couldn't have uprooted herself even if she had wanted to. She had to see his reaction; she had to try and discern his true feelings.

A swirl of blue silk flashed in the sunlight as the blonde woman flew down the steps.

"Amelia!" Ridge shouted, his arms outstretched.

The laughing woman flew into his arms and pressed her golden head against his shoulder. As she lifted her face to him and Ridge bent eagerly to kiss her, Deborah felt her heart shatter into a million pieces.

CHAPTER 11

DEBORAH WAS GRATEFUL for the happy reunion with the Warrens on the veranda. As they chatted and sipped tall glasses of lemonade, she was able to slip quietly into the house.

Once she reached the privacy of her room, Deborah locked both doors and flung herself on the narrow bed. She lay staring at the ceiling, too numb for anger or tears. A coldness encased her heart, like a block of ice, as she recalled the "perfect" couple downstairs.

Ridge's dark good looks provided the perfect foil for Amelia's golden beauty, just as her cultured background provided the right status for Ridge's ambitions—whatever they were. Adell obviously approved of the girl, had even gone to great lengths to promote this romance. No doubt, Stuart approved, since the older couple were life-long friends.

What did Ridge feel, she wondered suddenly.

The kiss had been short and brief, and she could not tell if it had been a kiss of friendship, or love. She recalled the words that had brought her such ecstasy only this morning: *I'm falling in love with you.*

Suddenly those words provided the shock she needed to jolt her back to her senses. Tears began to gather in her eyes as she thought about those words Ridge had spoken with such sincerity.

Falling in love . . . what did that mean? Was falling in and out of love just a passing infatuation to him compared to the deep love he might feel for Amelia? If he and Amelia had grown up together, perhaps he had always loved her. And yet he had said he had never been serious about a woman . . . "until you."

Deborah sat up on the bed, pushing a lock of hair from her face. She could not believe he intended to marry Amelia; he would not deceive her that way. She was suddenly certain of that fact. She had misjudged him before, without giving him a chance to explain. Now she was doing the same thing again, all because Adell was so adept at weaving her web of deceit. And this time she had help.

New hope beat in her heart as Deborah pulled herself up from the bed and began to pace the floor. Was she going to give up without a fight? Was she going to stand by, helplessly watching, while Amelia and Adell plotted? She had to be strong. She couldn't let doubt and lack of self-confidence convince her that she was unsuited for Ridge—not unless he told her so.

She washed her face, combed her hair, and sat down to her sewing, trying to calm herself. Perhaps she was jumping to conclusions after all, she thought, inserting a needle into a velvet cape.

Sometime later Torie popped into the sewing room, her eyes dancing with the excitement of company and festivities.

"We're going into town to have dinner," she said, fidgeting from one foot to the other. "Since the Warrens arrived a day early, there isn't enough time for Margarita to prepare the fancy banquet Mother wanted. So instead, we're going to an expensive restaurant in town. Are you coming with us?" She leaned down to peer into Deborah's face.

"I'm not acquainted with the Warrens," she answered in a noncommittal tone. "There's no reason for me to join you. And," she looked up, a twinkle in her eyes, "I think I'd be more comfortable here."

"I know what you mean," Torie studied her for a brief moment then leaned down to whisper in her ear. "I hate Amelia, don't you?"

Deborah's eyes widened on the girl's spiteful words. From the adjoining room, Amelia began to hum as she opened and closed drawers as she unpacked.

"You shouldn't say that, Torie," Deborah scolded softly.

"Well, I'm not a Christian like you. I can say anything I want to," she returned flippantly.

The tenseness that had settled between Deborah's shoulder blades had become a dull ache. And now Torie's careless remarks were adding to the strain she felt.

"After I go home, I want you to come visit me, Torie," she released a deep pent-up breath. "There are some things I cannot say to you now, but when I move home, I'll be able to speak freely."

"Mother probably won't let me come," Torie flounced into a chair, kicking at her trailing skirts. "She doesn't like you, you know."

The truth hurts, Deborah thought, wincing at the

child's bluntness. "Well, I suppose there's nothing I can do about that, Torie." She dropped her eyes to the cape in her lap, idly inserting the needle.

Footsteps sounded along the hall and Torie bolted from the chair.

"I'm supposed to be in my room getting ready," she called over her shoulder as she dashed from the room.

Deborah stared at the cape in her hands, the very last piece to be repaired unless, of course, the Warrens needed some mending.

Her hands grew idle as her mind wandered absently. How would she react if the young woman in the next room began tossing dresses her way? Her vision was filled with the memory of the beautiful woman and her fashionable clothing.

But she would not think of that now! She laid the cape aside and stood, flexing her muscles. Only a few days remained of her four week commitment here. To her surprise, she felt a strange sadness at the thought of leaving Cimarron. She wandered over to the narrow window and stared out across the green valley. Far in the distance, the vaqueros tended cattle; near the stable, some of the ranch hands were riding the mustangs brought in the day before. A sweet tangy odor filled the breeze, the odor of vine-ripened fruit at harvest, of rich earth, of cattle, horses, and sweet meadow grass.

She sighed, turning from the window. Was it this beautiful ranch she hated to leave—or was it Ridge? She knew the answer, of course.

A light tapping on her door stiffened her spine again. What now, she wondered, as she brushed a strand of dark hair from her forehead and crossed the room to open the door.

A gasp rose to her lips as her eyes met Ridge's handsome face. He was dressed in a dark broadcloth suit and ruffled white shirt. The smoky eyes deepened in an expression of happiness as he looked down at her.

"Deborah, I wish you could join us for dinner this evening," he said, clasping her hands in his.

For a moment, Deborah could only stare at him, her heart bursting with love. It seemed she loved him even more now that she sensed the threat of another woman.

"I hope you don't mind staying home alone," he continued at her silence. "Margarita will be here, of course."

She forced a smile, unaware that her hands were gripping his more tightly than before. "No, I'd rather stay here anyway."

He nodded, darting a glance down the hallway as though someone might be watching. "I hope you understand that while Amelia and the Warrens are here, I'm obligated to help entertain them."

No, she didn't understand, but what could she say?

He stepped inside the room and leaned down to press a kiss on her upturned cheek. "I'll see you later," he tapped her chin affectionately, then turned and quickly disappeared.

Obligated? she thought, turning the word over in her mind as though she had never heard it before. And she wondered what Amelia could do with that sense of obligation.

Deborah spent a sleepless night, tossing and turning in the narrow bed. She felt as though she were lying on a bed of stone, after the comfort of the soft feather mattress to which she had grown accustomed. But as she lay rigid, praying for sleep, she knew her discomfort stemmed from a problem far more complicated than the mattress beneath her.

Everyone arrived back home shortly before midnight. The sound of happy voices trailed through the house as Deborah stared into the darkness of her room. She could not cast aside the images that crowded into her mind—images of Amelia and Ridge smiling at one another throughout the evening, reliving joyous memories from the past.

When Deborah squeezed her dark lashes together in an effort to shut out those images, the lilting rhythm of Amelia's voice, cultured and charming, drifted through her consciousness. There was an easy confidence to her tone when she spoke to Stuart and Adell, a confidence that Deborah could not resist envying.

She is one of them, Deborah thought miserably. *I am not. I never can be.*

Like the fog rolling in from the ocean, cloaking shapes and textures, jealousy crept through her mind, obscuring logic and faith. Nothing was clear to her anymore; even the words that Ridge had spoken earlier, *I'm falling in love with you,* were fading in the flow of Amelia's overpowering presence.

"God, forgive me," she sobbed. "I don't want to have these feelings of jealousy and envy. But I can't help it."

Finally, as the cold light of dawn broke through her window, laying long gray fingers over her bed, exhaustion brought her a few hours of sleep.

Deborah's brave attempts to be polite to Amelia were met with cool indifference. The aristocratic young woman clearly considered Deborah a servant unworthy of her friendship. When, finally, Deborah's attempts at conversation were virtually ignored, she returned to her sewing room, vowing to say no more.

"I had an awful time in town last night," Torie grumbled as she slipped into Deborah's room and shut the door behind her.

"Why do you say that?" Deborah asked.

Torie shrugged, toying with the satin ribbon on her white dress. She had returned to formal dress again, and she was obviously uncomfortable. "The Warrens are boring—especially Amelia." Her blue eyes glinted angrily as she looked across at Deborah. "You know what they're trying to do, don't you?"

Deborah shrugged. "No."

"Amelia and Ridge. They're trying to match them up. It's been going on for years."

Deborah thrust her sewing aside and turned to Torie. "I need some fresh air. Want to come along?"

Torie and Deborah were just leaving the sewing room when the sound of Adell's sharp voice halted them. "Deborah, Miss Warren lost a button last night."

Deborah's frayed nerves began to snap. She lifted her chin and glared at Adell. She refused to be intimidated this time.

"Mother, we want to take a walk," Torie whined, her face tilted to study her mother anxiously. "Deborah can fix that button when we come back."

"I'd like her to do it *now*."

"I doubt that Miss Warren is planning to wear the same dress again today," Deborah said. "I'd appreciate some fresh air, if you don't mind." She turned to go.

"Just a minute!" Adell spoke harshly. "Torie, wait downstairs. I want to speak with Deborah privately."

Adell charged over to fling wide the door to the sewing room. Deborah hesitated for a fraction of a second, tempted to ignore her. But sensing Torie's lingering stare, she felt she would merely be setting a poor example for the girl. "I'll be down in a minute, Torie" she called lightly, adamant in her decision to go outside, despite Adell's rude behavior.

Once inside the sewing room, Adell slammed the door and thrust her hands on the hips of her new white dress. "I want Torie to become friends with Amelia." She glared at Deborah. "Obviously, she can't do that if you continue to monopolize her time."

"Monopolize her time?" Deborah repeated, her brows arched. "I've hardly seen Torie the past few days."

"Don't be difficult," Adell snapped. "Amelia and Ridge will be announcing wedding plans soon." She paused, apparently taking great satisfaction in the stunned expression on Deborah's face. "This is a very special time for both families. While you've been tolerant with Torie, I think it's time your little friendship ended. She has grown fond of you, and now I fear she won't be cordial to Amelia. And I don't want anything to ruin this special occasion." Adell folded her hands complacently before her, finishing her little speech with a look of smug triumph.

Deborah took a deep breath, reaching deep into her soul for strength she hadn't known she possessed. She decided to ignore the subject of wedding plans momentarily. Keeping her composure beneath this vindictive woman was more important than seeking answers.

"Mrs.. Farrington," she finally replied evenly, "Torie's attitude toward your guests does not concern me. I can't help it if she chooses to like or dislike anyone. What *does* concern me is your insinuation that I should hide in this room and play the part of an indentured servant. I have done good work for you— even *you* have admitted that. And now I feel the need to stretch my legs. If Torie wants to come along, she may."

"You're disappointed that your little scheme has failed, aren't you?" A malicious gleam lit Adell's faded blue eyes. "You hoped to capture Ridge for yourself, didn't you?"

Deborah fought valiantly against her rising temper. The one safeguard against losing it was the knowledge that it would please Adell to see her fall apart.

"I have entertained no such schemes. I do think it's rather odd that your son never mentioned his, er, *fiancée* in all of our conversations."

"They were not yet officially engaged," Adell retorted, her voice beginning to crack. "You *are* going to cause trouble, aren't you?" she asked, the pale lids slit as she studied Deborah angrily. "Let me remind you, Deborah, that your mother owes me a debt—"

"Which I have more than repaid!" Deborah replied, taking pride in the awareness that now she was behaving more rationally than Adell. "In fact, I'm more than willing to leave this very day if it will relieve your mind concerning my so-called schemes to hook your son."

"Not yet!" Adell huffed, the angry flush on her

cheeks now spreading across her face. "I want you here a while longer so that Ridge can make an intelligent comparison between you and Miss Warren. If you leave now, he's apt to be . . . suspicious. So I hope that you will stop being contrary; I wouldn't want to have to report your scandalous behavior while you've lived at Cimarron."

"What?" Deborah gasped, trying to imagine what she meant.

"You've disappeared into the darkness with my son on more than one occasion. Furthermore, I saw with my own eyes the two of you kissing and behaving shamefully on the veranda. The townspeople are inclined to forgive such behavior in a thirty-year-old man," Adell sneered, her eyes sweeping Deborah, "but not in *you*—the pious little seamstress's daughter! I greatly fear your mother's business will suffer once her customers hear of her daughter's shocking behavior, to say nothing of your impudence toward me."

Deborah could only stare, unable to believe her ears. It was hard to imagine that even Adell would stoop to such lies and deceit.

Suddenly, the door banged open and Torie stood before them, her face white, her tiny fists curled at her sides.

"No!" she cried out. "I heard what you said, and you can't do that to Deborah. Ridge won't let you." Her blue eyes flashed defiantly as she challenged her mother.

The sight of her distraught daughter shocked Adell into momentary silence. She stood wringing her hands, unable to frame a reply.

"I'm going downstairs to tell Ridge what you just said!" Torie yelled at her.

The threat jolted Adell into action.

"No, you aren't!" she hissed as Torie dashed out of the room. "Torie! Stop!"

Adell swung out the door after her.

Deborah followed, knowing there had to be a more rational way of handling this situation. "Torie, wait!" she called, as the little girl fled down the hall with Adell in close pursuit.

Before Deborah could catch up, a jagged scream ripped through the quiet house, a scream that accompanied the thud of Torie's frail little body as she tripped over her skirts and tumbled down the stairs.

Adell leaned over the banister, her eyes frozen in horror, her hands flying to her blue lips to silence the garbled screams.

Deborah pushed past her and paused at the top step, eyes widening in terror as she spotted Torie's crumpled body on the last step. "No!" she cried out. "No!"

Steps resounded on the marble tile as Stuart and Ridge bounded out of the parlor and cast a sweeping glance from Deborah and Adell at the top of the stairs, to Torie's lifeless body on the bottom step.

Stuart swore under his breath as his tear-filled eyes lifted again to his wife's frozen face.

Ridge knelt beside Torie, carefully examining a lump on the back of her head, and a cut from which blood was oozing.

Deborah clutched her skirt in white knuckled hands and descended the stairs on trembling legs. When she reached the bottom step, she knelt beside Ridge, her eyes blurred with tears as she caught sight of Torie's arm, twisted beneath her.

"Get the wagon!" Ridge yelled to Roberto, who

was standing in the front door. "We've got to get her to Los Angeles immediately." His gaze flew to the top step. "Mother, quick. Get bandages for her head."

"What happened?" Stuart asked hoarsely, quickly extracting his linen handkerchief to press to the back of Torie's head.

"It's all her fault!" Adell shrieked, awkwardly descending the stairs. "Deborah was arguing with Torie. Then Deborah started chasing her down the hall."

It took several seconds for Adell's words to penetrate Deborah's shocked senses, but the words began to register when she sensed all eyes upon her.

She lifted a stricken face to Adell's wild eyes. The shock she had just suffered was now compounded by Adell's murderous words. Surely in her state of shock, she had misunderstood what Adell said! Surely . . . she turned to Ridge, seeking reassurance.

But she met only horror in the grim face. And the eyes that had once adored her were now filled with contempt.

CHAPTER 12

DEBORAH WANDERED AIMLESSLY DOWN THE BOARD SIDE-
WALK. gazing absently at the awning overhanging the
hardware store. Her heart was as heavy as her steps,
but she knew that God's healing hand, in time, would
wipe away the heartbreak. The day was unseasonably
warm, driving Sonorans deeper into the shade of the
lemon trees and discouraging afternoon shoppers. Her
steps alone resounded on the wooden planks.

In the distance she could see the mustard-yellow
depot of the Southern Pacific where people milled
about, awaiting the next train. She stared at the train
tracks, which glinted in the afternoon sunlight. If not
for the Southern Pacific, she and her mother might
still be living in Kansas. And her father might still be
alive. She squeezed her dark lids together for a
moment, shutting out such useless thoughts.

Suddenly an intense ache for her old home and
friends filled her heart, and she swallowed against the
hard lump in her throat. If only she could turn back

the clock and be a little girl again, playing about her father's store, sampling peppermint sticks and admiring the China dolls. But there was no going back. God had a plan for her life, and she must seek His will, even though she saw no purpose in her association with the Farringtons. All she felt when she thought of them was pain, intense pain.

She blinked against the hard glare of the sun, slashing down the boardwalk, filling her eyes, and increasing the dull ache in her head. The clanging of the trolley car grated on her nerves, and she had a foolish desire to lift her hands to her ears to shut out that sound. But someone might think she had gone mad, she thought with a bitter grin; particularly when they looked into her sad, hollow eyes.

God help me, she silently begged as she stopped at the corner, gazing through tears to the hospital across the street. It was all she could do to keep from pushing through the door to seek out a doctor, a nurse, anyone who could tell her if Torie were alive or dead. But a glimpse of her in the corridor might send Adell into another fit of hysteria.

Deborah bit her lip, trying again to blot out the hideous accusation Adell had made. She could not think of that now, not while she stood on a street corner, ready to burst into tears.

She swung around and directed her steps toward the community church at the end of the street. She would go there to pray, as she had done the evening before. It was the only way she had been able to find any measure of peace.

The nightmare of the day before had taken on an eerie quality in her mind. When she recalled the events that had occurred, it was as though she looked through a distorted mirror, seeing nothing clearly.

157

After Ridge and Roberto had prepared a bed in the back of the buckboard and carefully placed Torie's limp body there, they had hurried off to town without a word to her. Stuart and Adell had followed in the family carriage, their faces set grimly. Deborah, seated in a rickety old wagon, had been delivered to her mother's doorstep by a sad old Spaniard.

If only she hadn't argued with Adell, she thought miserably; if only she had gone along with the woman's suggestion, the accident might not have happened.

While one part of her mind argued the logic of her reasoning, she still could not escape a small measure of guilt. Her sad eyes lifted to the whitewashed adobe church before her, the open door beckoning to all. Her steps quickened as she entered the small, square building where several rows of wooden benches led to a tiny altar. The mellow dimness of the church washed over her, offering relief from the burning sun, soothing the deep pain in her heart.

A candle flickered on the small oak table at the altar, and she pushed her weary body up the narrow aisle to the light. As she glanced about the church, she was relieved to see that she was alone. She needed privacy for this special talk with God.

Slowly, she dropped to her knees before the altar, her eyes fixed on the Cross above her. For a moment, she scarcely moved as she drank in the peace that seemed to flow down to her from that small wooden Cross, where another, so long ago, had suffered and died. How thankful she should be that she had come to know this One at an early age, and that she, unlike the woman who had treated her so cruelly, could turn to this Being now for strength and comfort.

Deborah pressed her palms together, staring thoughtfully at the Cross. She would never understand the painful events that had taken place, yet the deep faith that had been instilled in her since birth was vibrant within her now. She could feel the heavy burden in her heart begin to lift. She lowered her head and closed her eyes; then softly she began to pray. She had no idea how long she had been kneeling there, praying for Torie's recovery, when she heard footsteps and sensed someone standing directly behind her.

The skin on her neck prickled, as she opened her eyes and slowly turned her head. She met a pair of smoky eyes, hollow and pain-filled.

A tremulous smile touched her lips. "Ridge," she whispered.

He stood in the shadows watching her intently, his trousers and shirt wrinkled, his face haggard and slightly bearded.

"How is she?" Deborah asked, her breath caught in her throat as she awaited the answer.

He dropped to his knees beside her and shook his head, unable to reply.

Horror clutched at her heart as she imagined the worst. "Is she . . ." her lips froze on the words.

"She's barely hanging on," he replied hoarsely, his eyes lifted to the Cross.

But at least she's alive, Deborah thought, hope flaring in her anew. As long as there was breath in her little body, there was hope.

Ridge's hollow eyes moved to Deborah. "Maybe here I can pray," he said humbly. "Somehow I've not been able to find the right words."

Deborah nodded, instinctively reaching for his

hand. For the first time since she had known him, his hand was cold, lifeless, devoid of the strength he had so often pressed into her own fingers. She turned back to the altar and closed her eyes.

"Dear God," she said quietly, "please hear our prayer . . ." Her words drifted upward peacefully as she offered a plea for Torie's life. As she spoke the words, new strength seemed to flow through her body, touching her voice, filling her with firm conviction. Finally, when her prayer ended, she felt the soft pressure of Ridge's hand on hers.

"Come with me," he said, helping her to her feet. "The doctor has said her chances of surviving will be much greater if she can only regain consciousness. Maybe your presence there . . ."

Deborah bit her lip, wondering what Adell's reaction would be if she came to the hospital. But the person to consider now was Torie. She couldn't let pride interfere if there was anything she could do to help.

"Of course," she said, answering the desperate plea in his eyes.

Neither spoke as they hurried back to the hospital. As they turned down the corridor to Torie's room, Deborah's eyes met the puzzled faces of Stuart and Adell. They were standing in the hall, a look of despair in their hollow eyes.

"Come on," Ridge urged softly, pressing his hand to her back.

Adell's eyes widened on Deborah before she swung around and walked to the end of the hall to stare through a narrow window.

Deborah took a deep breath, forcing herself to hurry on. As they reached the door to Torie's room,

Stuart stepped forward, his hand extended to Deborah in a greeting. She looked up into the sad, dark face and her heart wrenched within her at the sight of his pain.

"Hello, Deborah." He nodded politely. His voice was kind, the smile sincere.

"Hello, Mr. Farrington," she smiled at him, aware that he, like Ridge, must have chosen to disbelieve his wife's cruel story. Otherwise, he could not treat her with such kindness. "Thank you for coming," he said, glancing back at the door to Torie's room. "Perhaps your prayers will be heard. . . ." His bleak eyes looked to the floor.

Deborah swallowed, unable to reply. Ridge was tugging at her arm, leading her inside the room. A gasp escaped her as her eyes flew to the bed where Torie lay. Her head and arm were heavily bandaged, and her face appeared bloodless. Her small features had taken on a pinched expression, as though she were fighting the pain.

Suddenly fear clutched at Deborah's heart, challenging the strong sense of victory she had felt back at the church. No, she would not weaken, she told herself, staring at the still, frail form. Torie was going to live. She had felt that assurance minutes before, and she would not allow doubts to discourage her.

As she approached the bed, she reached out and took Torie's small hand in hers; it was cold and lifeless. For a moment, she could only stare, scarcely believing the little girl who had been so much a part of her life the past weeks now hovered on the brink of death.

Deborah lifted the hand to her lips and pressed a kiss onto the slim fingers. Clutching Torie's hand, she began to pray.

Seconds slipped into minutes; minutes stretched on as she continued to pray softly, oblivious to all else.

Sometime later she felt a small finger twitching against her palm. Deborah ceased praying and opened her eyes to study the little girl. The face was still, yet the finger twitched again. The hand moved. Deborah watched, her breath caught in her throat. Slowly, the pale lashes began to flutter.

"Torie? Torie?" Deborah bent over the child, her voice and her eyes compelling the child to respond.

Torie's pale lashes fluttered again, and slowly, ever so slowly, her eyes opened.

"Torie!" Deborah cried out, unable to restrain herself.

She felt Ridge's arm on her shoulder as he leaned over his sister, softly calling her name.

The pale blue eyes stared blankly at the ceiling.

"I'll get Mother and Father," Ridge whispered, squeezing Deborah's arm before he left.

"Torie, it's me. Deborah." She gently rubbed the child's hand, her breath lodged in her chest as she waited for Torie to respond.

Slowly, the blank gaze moved toward the sound of Deborah's voice, and then the pale lips quivered in an effort to smile.

"I . . . saw Him." The voice was a thin whisper. Her lashes drooped, as though the effort to speak had exhausted her.

"Tell me about it, Torie," she pressed the child's hand again, knowing she must keep her awake.

Stuart and Adell rushed into the room, a doctor close behind.

"Deborah, I saw Him," Torie repeated. "He reached out to me . . . but then I woke up."

No one moved.

"Torie, you're going to be all right," Deborah said, tears of joy spilling from her eyes. She could feel the others crowding around the bed.

The doctor had emerged to study the child with a bright, pleased smile. He winked at Deborah as he took Torie's pulse and observed her thoughtfully.

Deborah stepped back from the bed, offering a quick smile to Stuart who was staring wide-eyed at his daughter. Adell's attention was focused on the doctor as she avoided Deborah's fleeting glance.

She slipped out of the room and looked up and down the hall. Ridge was nowhere to be seen. Quietly, she walked away. Torie would recover! She felt certain of that now.

"Deborah, what's wrong?" Maggie Holt frowned across their small living room. "You've hardly spoken a word all day."

Deborah lifted blank eyes from the book in her hand. The words of the page meant nothing to her, but reading had been an attempt to divert her thoughts. "I'm sorry, Mother," Deborah laid the book aside and released a heavy sigh. "I was just thinking about something."

"About Ridge Farrington?" her mother asked, studying her daughter's downcast face.

"No, actually I was thinking about Torie," Deborah replied, staring absently out the window.

"Why didn't you ever go back to the hospital to see Torie, dear?" she asked gently. "You were her friend. You had a right to be there."

Deborah swung her bare feet under her and leaned her dark head against the chair. "I know," she said. "But I didn't want to cause problems."

Maggie studied her silent daughter for a moment, then pulled herself wearily from the settee and went into the kitchen to place the tea kettle on the burner. She, like her daughter, appeared to be deep in thought as she prepared tea for the two of them. When she returned to the living room, with the tray, she looked at Deborah with an exasperated sigh.

"Frankly, dear, I don't think the Farringtons treated you fairly," she said, pouring tea. "Well, perhaps Ridge did, but I still think he should have come to report Torie's progress. It seemed, well, inconsiderate of them not to let you know of her recovery. Imagine having to hear about it through a customer."

"It doesn't matter, Mother. Ridge owes me no explanations. We were . . . only friends." She busied herself with the tea cup.

Maggie's eyes reflected the pain she had shared with her daughter the past days. "Darling, I know you too well," she said gently. "There's no point in trying to hide the truth from me." She paused, sipping her tea. At her daughter's lengthy silence, Maggie placed her tea cup on the table and turned back with a compassionate smile. "You're in love with Ridge Farrington, aren't you?"

Deborah pondered the question as she looked back out the living room window, her gaze following the curl of steam from the Chinese laundry across the street.

"Yes, I am in love with him," she admitted, with an ache in her throat. "But what good will it ever do me? We're all wrong for each other." She took a long, deep breath and turned sad eyes to her mother. "We come from entirely different backgrounds. Despite

164

Ridge's interest in me, I'm certain he realizes that a girl like," she swallowed, "Amelia Warren is a better match than I am."

"But Deborah, the choice is his! You can't make assumptions as to what he should or shouldn't do. I think character is—"

Deborah interrupted her. "Please, Mother, let's not discuss it. Ridge and I have nothing in common except our faith—and we have a different approach even in that respect. If Torie were my little sister, I would try to witness to her. Ridge never has."

Maggie was silent for a moment, then she reached across to clasp her daughter's hand. "Perhaps some good will come of all this. It's too soon to tell. In time, I believe that God will heal your hurt, dear."

Deborah nodded, unable to respond, as she leaned forward to press a kiss on her mother's cheek. "It's been a long day, Mother. I think I'll go to bed."

Sadly, Maggie watched Deborah leave. Her daughter's heart was breaking and there was nothing she could do. Nothing except pray. But perhaps that was all anyone could do.

CHAPTER 13

A COOLING BREEZE whispered through the palms along Spring Street, drifting through the open window of the sewing shop.

Deborah hummed softly to herself as she stepped back from the worktable to study the broadcloth riding habit she was designing. The door opened, ringing the chime overhead. Deborah looked up, thinking Mrs. Williams was early for her fitting.

The doorway was filled with the large frame of Ridge Farrington. He seemed taller, or perhaps it was merely because he looked so out of place in their small, feminine shop. In the two weeks since she had seen him he had lost weight, deepening the lines in his bronzed face.

"Hello, Deborah." He removed his derby and stood absently twirling it in his suntanned hands.

"Hello," she smiled, staring into the eyes that were as gray as the evening mist.

A tense silence followed. Ridge turned to glance about the sewing shop.

Deborah followed his gaze, trying to see their shop through his eyes. Bolts of bright silk, sateen, and taffeta lined the counter, along with calico, cotton and muslin. The shop was not fancy, yet it offered a homey atmosphere and suggested a flourishing business.

"It's small but serviceable," she looked back at him. "How is Torie?"

"She's getting along fine." Their gazes locked and he took a step closer. "Deborah, I must talk to you." A haunted look surfaced in the dark eyes.

Her pulse was throbbing erratically but she tried to conceal her jittery nerves behind a quick smile. "Then do sit down," she motioned to a chair.

He merely glanced at the chair and continued to twirl his hat. He was obviously too nervous to sit, Deborah decided, as she crossed her arms and leaned against the counter, waiting.

"I hardly know where to begin," he said, suddenly avoiding her eyes.

"Would you like a cup of tea?" she asked.

"No." His eyes flickered toward hers. "I'd like you to come back to Cimarron with me."

"I beg your pardon?" Deborah said, grasping the counter to support herself.

"Please come out to Cimarron. Torie wants to see you." He hesitated for a moment. "And my mother wants very much to speak with you."

Deborah blinked in confusion. "I would like to see Torie," she managed to reply. "I've been very concerned about her. And I'm sorry you didn't bother to let me know how she was doing."

He lifted a hand to rake distractedly through his dark curls. "So much happened at once," he sighed.

"My father was summoned to San Francisco for an important vote at a stockholders' meeting. Naturally, he didn't want to leave while Torie's condition was so critical, so I went in his place. On the day I returned from San Francisco, Torie was released from the hospital. That same day my mother had a heart attack."

"What? I hadn't heard about that."

"No," he said, "we kept it fairly quiet. She didn't want to be bothered with visitors inquiring about her health."

"Oh, Ridge." She shook her head sympathetically. "You've had one problem after another, haven't you?"

He lifted his face to stare at her, puzzled. "Deborah," he finally responded, "how could you feel compassion toward any of us? I know you can never forgive us for the way we treated you." A look of torment clouded his eyes.

"Never forgive you?" she repeated, frowning.

"We behaved like monsters. Mother's cruel accusation was unforgivable. And I didn't defend you that day, even though I knew Torie's accident couldn't possibly be your fault. It was just that, well," he shook his head in frustration, "in the beginning it was hard to believe my mother would tell an outright lie about something so serious. As soon as my head cleared I knew you could never do anything to harm Torie." He turned from her and began to pace the floor. "On the day I came to the church and asked you to return with me to the hospital, I didn't even apologize to you for not defending you that day. There were so many things I wanted to say to you, but Torie's condition overshadowed all else at the time.

After she came out of the coma, I returned to Cimarron to let our guests know the schedule for departing trains."

He broke off, staring at Deborah for a long moment.

"And I also wanted to end the subterfuge between Amelia and myself. I never felt anything for Amelia other than a deep, childhood friendship. I'm sorry if you were led to believe otherwise."

Deborah took a deep breath. "It's all right, Ridge. Let's just try to forget about what has happened and go on with our lives."

"Come home with me." He reached out to grip her hand. "Please. We have to talk. And Torie would be so happy to see you."

Deborah stiffened at the prospect of returning to Cimarron. She remembered the tragic departure and the old hurt stabbed her again. But if it would make Torie happy? And this would only be for a visit, she reminded herself. Surely she could tolerate a quick visit, she decided, her heart softening at the urgent plea in Ridge's voice.

"I'll come," she told him. "But I'll have to wait until Mother returns from the laundry. There's no one else to mind the shop."

"We'll wait as long as you wish. Juan and the carriage are at our disposal."

Later, as Deborah rode to Cimarron with Ridge, her thoughts drifted back to her first ride in the family carriage. Her eyes slipped across to Ridge, staring at the distant foothills, lost in his own thoughts. So much had happened during the past weeks; she wondered now if she or the Farringtons would ever be the same.

Suddenly he turned and met her searching look and an expression of tenderness softened his bronzed face. "What are you thinking?" he asked.

She glanced toward the grazing cattle that filled the meadows of Cimarron. "I've been thinking about my first trip to Cimarron, and particularly my first glimpse of you. You were branding cattle that day."

"Ah yes," he lifted a hand to stroke his jaw. "Mother told me recently that you thought I was a cruel person to apply a branding iron to an innocent little calf."

She laughed softly. "Only because I didn't understand cattle branding," she replied.

His eyes swept over her slowly. "You're wearing the same green dress you wore that day."

Her brows arched in surprise. "You remember?"

"How could I forget? I looked up from the calf with perspiration dripping down my face and discovered the loveliest vision of green I'd ever seen. And I wondered at my good fortune on seeing you in our carriage."

Her smile faded, as she remembered her reason for being in the carriage. Slowly, she pulled her eyes from his, and turned back to the window. As always, Adell had thrust a barrier between them. This time it was only a memory, yet it was real enough to discourage Deborah from losing sight of the real problem.

"Why does your mother want to see me?" she asked dully.

He hesitated. "I think it's better to let her speak for herself," he finally replied.

Deborah fidgeted against the velvet cushions, wondering if she could possibly endure any more of his mother's insults. This time she wouldn't have to stay for them, she reminded herself.

Suddenly an unpleasant thought nudged its way into her moment of satisfaction. What if she intended to threaten her again? What if she wanted her to come back to work for her?

"Stop worrying," Ridge reached across to clasp her hand. "This is going to be a pleasant visit. You have my word, Deborah."

She turned troubled eyes to his, knowing he could not possibly understand the lengths to which his mother would go to keep them apart, but she said nothing. Instead, she pushed a brave smile onto her lips.

"I do hope that Torie is going to recover fully," she said, remembering Ridge's earlier comments about her progress.

"She's fine. Although she suffered a severe concussion, excellent medical care and proper rest have worked a miracle. Or maybe it was your prayer." He lifted her hand to his lips, kissing each finger tip.

"Ridge, please don't," she said, withdrawing her hand. He made her uncomfortable now when he looked at her in the old way, more uncomfortable still when he touched her.

"Deborah," he scooted to the edge of the seat, "Torie had some sort of vision while she was in a coma. She thought she was with God. She's been different every since she regained consciousness."

"Different?" Deborah asked. "How?"

A thoughtful expression crossed his face as he glanced out the window for a second. "She's been kinder." He looked back at Deborah. "Sweeter. I'm certain that she now believes in God."

"Well," Deborah smiled, releasing the breath she hadn't known she was holding, "maybe some good has come of this, after all. I'm just sorry that Torie had to suffer."

"Torie isn't the only one who suffered," he said quietly.

The carriage was turning into the driveway leading up to the house. When Deborah saw it, a wave of conflicting emotions assailed her. Anxiety, regret and . . . happiness meshed into a bittersweet nostalgia as she stared through the leafy branches to the red roof glinting in the afternoon sunshine. To her utter astonishment, she realized that she had missed this ranch; it had managed to claim a special place in her heart, despite the turmoil and unpleasantness.

There *were* some good times, she reminded herself, as the carriage rolled to a halt in the graveled drive. Suddenly, the door was being opened and Roberto's dark shining eyes greeted her. A wide, eager smile lit his face.

"Miss Holt!" He bobbed a courteous nod. "Welcome."

"Thank you, Roberto," she said, taking the hand he offered to assist her from the carriage.

"Deborah!"

Torie's eager voice reached her and she spun around, glancing toward the veranda where Torie was propped up in a swing.

Deborah hurried up the walk to the veranda, her arms outstretched to Torie.

"Oh Torie! It's so good to see you," she cried, hugging the child to her. As Deborah's fingers touched the girl's jutting shoulder blades, she realized she had lost far too much weight, when she had already been too thin. She leaned back to look down into Torie's pale, gaunt face. The blue eyes were bright and eager, the small mouth was spread in a pleased smile.

"Torie, you look pretty," Deborah said, her eyes

sailing over the casual cotton dress. "I've never seen your hair without the braid." She smiled, eyeing the golden hair that swung freely about her shoulders. Was it her hair, or the deeper wisdom in her blue eyes that suddenly made Torie seem older, Deborah wondered.

"Maybe I've outgrown the braid," Torie grinned, squeezing her arm. "Thanks for coming to see me."

"I've been dying to see you," Deborah hugged her again. "How are you feeling?"

"Better. And I have lots to tell you," she said, her eyes darting over Deborah's shoulder to Ridge. Deborah glanced back with a grin, sensing that Torie would wait until they could speak privately.

"First, let's go up and see Mother," Ridge nudged Deborah. "Then you two can chat to your hearts' content."

Deborah stiffened in spite of her resolve. She tried to muster up some enthusiasm as she straightened, but it was impossible.

"She's been confined to her bed since the heart attack," Ridge explained as they entered the dim hallway.

"Where's Margarita?" Deborah sniffed, noticing the absence of the usual pleasant aromas drifting out of the kitchen.

"Unfortunately, she's gone to visit a sick relative. She'll be sorry she missed you."

As they approached the stairway, a sick feeling gripped Deborah's stomach as her eyes dropped to the bottom stair. She tried to shut out the horrible memory of Torie's little body, lying twisted on the stairs, but that was impossible, too. The vivid scene was still fresh in her mind.

Ridge looked down at her, suddenly sensing her discomfort. He slipped his arm about her waist, guiding her gently up the step. At his touch, she darted a questioning glance up at him and saw an expression on his face that made her heart beat faster. *Did he still care for her?* she asked herself for the hundredth time since he had appeared in the shop that afternoon. The intense look in his eye held something far deeper than friendship, but this time she would not delude herself in believing she had a chance with him. There was no point in even hoping until she knew what Adell was going to say to her.

As they reached the upper level, Deborah's eyes scanned the hall, pausing on the closed door to the room that had been hers, then Amelia Warren's. A deep sigh was squeezed from her tight chest as she recalled the beautiful young woman. She found it hard to believe that Ridge could not love a woman like that! But perhaps her mother had been right; perhaps he was more concerned with character than beauty. . . .

Their steps halted before the door to a room that Deborah had never entered. Not once during her stay at Cimarron had she been invited to Adell's private quarters.

Deborah felt another pang of dread as Ridge knocked softly on the door. She sank her teeth into her lower lip, wondering if she could possibly be polite to the woman who had hurt her so.

A muffled reply answered the knock as Ridge turned the knob and slowly pushed the door open. Deborah froze in the doorway, then she felt the gentle pressure of Ridge's hand on her shoulder, and with a deep strengthening breath, she thrust her chin up and entered the room.

The luxurious room was decorated in shades of blue and peach, and filled with beautiful antiques. Guardedly, her eyes crept across to the large, four-poster bed . . . and the still woman who seemed to have sunk into the feather mattress.

Deborah never imagined it possible for Adell Farrington to appear vulnerable. But the pallor of her skin, the disorderly tangle of her hair, and the sagging face stripped her of the formidable appearance she had always maintained. She was clearly a sick, helpless woman who had aged at least ten years in the past two weeks! The protruding blue eyes that had chipped away at Deborah during those difficult weeks now held a look of weary defeat.

"Come in, Deborah." Even the voice was frail and weak.

"Hello, Mrs. Farrington." Deborah pushed a tiny smile onto her face as she crept toward the bed.

"Ridge, pull up a chair for her," Adell gave her son a weak smile. "And if you don't mind, I'd like to speak privately with Deborah."

Ridge hesitated by Deborah's chair, obviously reluctant to leave. Then, he nodded and glanced down at Deborah. "After you talk with Mother, I'd like us to take a ride out to Sunset Point."

Deborah held her breath, trying to frame a tactful refusal.

"That would be nice," Adell agreed. "You two should do that." Her gray lips trembled in a half smile.

Deborah leaned back in the chair, stunned, only vaguely aware of Ridge's departing steps. Adell's attitude appeared to be as drastically changed as her health—but was she sincere? Or what this just another ploy to make Deborah look foolish? She folded her hands in her lap, waiting for the woman to speak her mind.

Adell spoke with great effort. "I appreciate your coming."

Deborah could see that conversation was a strain for her, and despite her bitterness, Deborah felt concern. "I'm sorry to hear of your illness," she said.

"Thank you," Adell murmured. "The doctor said I should stay in bed for a while. Stuart is quite adamant that I do so." A wistful expression crossed her face. "I suppose my illness has awakened his protective urges again." She took a deep breath and studied her large hands, folded across the bosom of her blue satin gown. "I'm afraid our marriage has been far from ideal. I'm largely to blame for that."

Her eyes shifted from the blue-purple veins in her hands to Deborah's curious face.

"I'm trying to make amends for a lot of things," she continued. "Torie's accident made me see how quickly a life can be snatched away, and the regrets that can fill one's heart at such a time."

She paused to still her labored breathing. Deborah's nervous fingers gripped the arm of the chair, as her muscles tensed anxiously.

"When my heart acted up, it gave us all a scare," Adell said. "I've had plenty of time to think lately, and one thing that continues to haunt me is the way I treated you and your mother." She turned sad eyes to Deborah. "I wouldn't want to die with that on my conscience."

Deborah swallowed, searching her mind for the right words. "Mrs. Farrington, you aren't going to die. I'm certain—"

"I don't plan to," she interrupted, "but all the same I'd like to clear the slate if it's not too late. Deborah," she took a deep breath and shook her silver head. "I treated you very badly and I'm so ashamed. You see," her eyes swept Deborah thoughtfully, "I envied you and your mother from the very first day I walked into your sewing shop."

"You *envied*?" Deborah repeated, startled by this admission.

Adell nodded. "I overheard your mother speaking with another customer about her faith, and that she and her daughter would survive in their strange new home." Adell's eyes roamed toward the window. "Those words awakened a sense of guilt in me," she said in a thin voice. "I looked around the sewing shop and saw your ingenuity and talent. I looked into your mother's face and saw a radiance and joy that had always been missing in my life. I have made all sorts of excuses for my misery—my rather plain looks, the fact that I had been uprooted and moved out here where I knew no one."

She looked back at Deborah and smiled. "Then I met a woman who had little materially, and no one to love except her daughter. Yet, she had something my money could not buy! I was suddenly filled with hate, a hate I could neither understand nor justify. I wanted to prove that this radiance of hers was all an act, that she was not as strong as she appeared to be. That this God of hers was not capable of bringing such happiness . . ." her words faltered as tears sprang into her eyes.

The tears, as much as the words, shocked Deborah into speechlessness. She wanted to make some consoling comment, but she was beyond words. Then, unable to offer any type of verbal comfort, she merely reached forward and clasped the woman's hand.

Adell gave her a bitter smile. "Wait. You haven't heard the worst. And it is so difficult for me to tell you this."

"Then don't." Deborah found her voice at last. "You've said enough, Mrs. Farrington. I think I understand."

"No." A bitter laugh escaped her. "I must tell you this. You see," she gave Deborah a long, measuring stare, "I was the one who knocked the inkwell onto the dress, not your mother."

Deborah thought she was incapable of further shock, but suddenly her mind was reeling again.

"I knew no alterations could make the gown accommodate the extra pounds I had gained," she continued, weak but determined. "I hated my fat figure, and I hated your mother for her beauty, her poise, her ability to handle every crisis with grace. My marriage was disintegrating and I was miserable. Suddenly your mother became a target for my wrath. I wanted to wipe that complacent smile from her face, prove that no one was as strong as she pretended to be. Then, when you came to Cimarron, I repeated the injustice on you."

Deborah's feelings changed from disbelief to awe and finally acceptance of the truth.

"I know now," Adell conceded, "that your mother is genuine and so are you. You are the kindest, most loving person I have ever known."

Deborah's eyes dropped to the hand that she was holding, but there was no strength in the hand. *What do I feel*, she wondered numbly. *Why don't I hate her? I'm not even angry with her!*

178

Her eyes rose slowly to the sagging face on the pillow, and Deborah realized that the only feeling in her heart was pity for a woman who had wasted so much of her life, and whose unhappiness had brought misery to others, as well.

"It took great courage for you to admit this," Deborah heard herself speaking words she hadn't known she would say. "I respect you for that, Mrs. Farrington."

"The weeks you spent here were the happiest of Torie's life," Adell continued, as though she hadn't heard Deborah. "You showed her love and happiness and strength by your own example. And you've been good for Ridge," she admitted, the wistfulness returning to her face. "He loves you, Deborah. I only hope you love him, too. And if it isn't asking too much, I beg you to forgive me."

The tears that had gathered in Adell's eyes earlier now slipped down over the thin lashes. "Later when I'm stronger," she said through quivering lips, "I intend to go to your mother and ask her forgiveness as well. In the meantime, maybe you can tell me about this loving God of yours   who Torie says can forgive someone as unlovable as me."

"No one is unforgivable or unlovable," Deborah said on a shaky breath. A lump had lodged in her throat, making each word an effort. "He will forgive you, and certainly I accept your apology. The important thing now," she swallowed, "is for you to forgive yourself. And get well," she added with an encouraging smile. "Perhaps we can ask my minister to come out and talk with you."

A soft knock interrupted their conversation and Deborah glanced toward the door. Adell clutched at her hand, her eyes filled with desperation.

"Have we made our peace?" she asked.

"Yes, of course we have," Deborah answered.

"Good." A deep trembling sigh was heaved from her chest as her features softened in relief. "And I want you to know that you and Ridge have my blessings," she added softly.

The door was opening and Ridge stepped into the room, glancing quickly from one woman to the other, obviously searching for clues to the outcome of their conversation.

Deborah offered him a reassuring smile, one that immediately lit his face with happiness. "Torie has gone to her bedroom looking for the checkerboard," he said. "I'm afraid you're in for a real match—after our ride."

"Come back to see me," Adell smiled as Deborah stood up.

"Yes, I will," she nodded. "Hurry and get well."

Neither she nor Ridge spoke as they descended the stairs. Deborah tried to absorb the shock of Adell's confession, but she was still walking as though in a dream. *A dream,* she repeated the words in her mind. How many nights had she lain awake imagining herself back at Cimarron with Ridge, pretending that there were no obstacles to their love.

With a look of awe, she turned her face slowly to stare at Ridge. It was no longer a dream. It had really happened.

Ridge caught her astonished glance and stopped midway down the steps. "What are you thinking?" he asked.

She shook her head, trying to clear the confusion from her mind. "I guess I'm just experiencing the joy of answered prayer," she said, as they continued on

180

again. "Ridge, your mother and I have made our peace."

He lifted a hand to squeeze the fingers that gripped his arm. "She's changed, Deborah. I could have told you that, but I wanted you to see for yourself. And all she could talk about lately was the need to speak with you. It's been like an obsession with her."

Deborah nodded, as they reached the bottom step and turned up the hall to the front veranda.

"But now that we've cleared up the misunderstandings, I think it's time we celebrated."

Deborah turned inquisitive eyes to him, as he pushed the front door open and they stepped onto the deserted veranda.

"What are we celebrating?" she asked, smiling up into his face. "There have been so many blessings today."

"Perhaps the greatest is yet to come," he said, lifting her fingers to his lips to press kisses into her hand. "Deborah, I love you with all of my heart," he confessed, adoring her with his eyes. "You belong here with me. Well, not *here*," he glanced about the veranda. "When we ride out to Sunset Point, you can choose the perfect spot for our home. Will you marry me?"

His words left her too breathless to reply for a moment.

Then, with a toss of her dark head, her green eyes widened in her delicate face. "Ridge, I don't know how many more surprises I can take in one day!"

Before she could say more, Ridge lowered his head and brushed his lips over her forehead, down the tip of her nose, and finally her lips. Slowly, her arms crept up his arms, resting on his shoulders as he pulled her against his chest and kissed her with a deep and tender yearning.

As she responded to his kiss, the world began to spin again, this time in a wonderful way.

Frightened by the intensity of her feelings, she pulled her head back and tried to catch her breath. "Please, Ridge," she laughed softly, "you're making me absolutely dizzy!"

He chuckled, pleased to know that he affected her so. "Deborah," a frown pulled his dark brows together, "you've never told me you loved me, but I dared hope."

"Yes, I do love you," she admitted with a sigh. "I think I loved you from the first moment I saw you. Out there," she motioned toward the valley, "with your hat slouched over those pretty curls." She lifted a finger to tug at a toppling strand. "I looked into your eyes and . . . something happened." Her teasing smile faded into a serious expression. "I could never be the same again."

"Nor could I." He slipped his arm around her shoulder, guiding her gently across the veranda to the front step. "The only thing that comes close to affecting me half as much as you is this land—" he lifted an arm to sweep the air while he spoke, "—and the sunsets over the valley."

Deborah nodded in comprehension, turning her face to the horizon where the setting sun cast fiery splendor across the fields.

"We'll build a good life here, Deborah." Ridge's voice was husky with emotion.

"Yes," she nodded thoughtfully, "we will."

Arm in arm, they turned and walked toward the stable, their silhouettes outlined in the sun's streaming rays.

ABOUT THE AUTHOR

PEGGY DARTY, a former advertising and public relations copywriter, is now a full-time author. CIM-ARRON SUNSET is her third novel for Serenade, following the award-winning A MOUNTAIN TO STAND STRONG, and KINCAID OF CRIPPLE CREEK. Her works have also been published by Bantam Books, *Parents Magazine*, *Lady's Circle*, *Home Life*, and others. She and her husband, Landon, reside in Jasper, Alabama, with their three children. It is Mrs. Darty's primary objective to present real-life characters who overcome obstacles through faith and love, and to inspire readers with the eternal significance of hope.

A Letter To Our Readers

Dear Reader:

Welcome to the world of Serenade Books—a series designed to bring you the most beautiful love stories in the world of inspirational romance. They will uplift you, encourage you, and provide hours of wholesome entertainment, so thousands of readers have testified. In order that we might better contribute to your reading enjoyment, we would appreciate your taking a few minutes to respond to the following questions and return to:

> Editor, Serenade Books
> The Zondervan Publishing House
> 1415 Lake Drive, S.E.
> Grand Rapids, Michigan   49506

1. Did you enjoy reading CIMARRON SUNSET?

   ☐ Very much. I would like to see more books by this author!
   ☐ Moderately
   ☐ I would have enjoyed it more if _____

2. Where did you purchase this book? _____

3. What influenced your decision to purchase this book?

   ☐ Cover   ☐ Back cover copy
   ☐ Title   ☐ Friends
   ☐ Publicity   ☐ Other _____

4. What are some inspirational themes you would like to see treated in future books?

_____

5. Please indicate your age range:
   ☐ Under 18   ☐ 25–34   ☐ 46–55
   ☐ 18–24   ☐ 35–45   ☐ Over 55

6. If you are interested in receiving information about our Serenade Home Reader Service, in which you will be offered new and exciting novels on a regular basis, please give us your name and address. (This does NOT obligate you for membership.)

   Name _____

   Occupation _____

   Address _____

   City _____ State _____ Zip _____

Serenade Saga books are inspirational romances in historical settings, designed to bring you a joyful, heart-lifting reading experience.

Serenade Saga books available in your local book store:

Serenade Serenata books are inspirational romances in contemporary settings, designed to bring you a joyful, heart-lifting reading experience.

Serenade Serenata books available in your local bookstore:

#1 On Wings of Love, Elaine L. Schulte
#2 Love's Sweet Promise, Susan C. Feldhake
#3 For Love Along, Susan C. Feldhake
#4 Love's Late Spring, Lydia Heermann
#5 In Comes Love, Mab Graff Hoover
#6 Fountain of Love, Velma S. Daniels and Peggy E. King.
#7 Morning Song, Linda Herring
#8 A Mountain to Stand Strong, Peggy Darty
#9 Love's Perfect Image, Judy Baer
#10 Smoky Mountain Sunrise, Yvonne Lehman
#11 Greengold Autumn, Donna Fletcher Crow
#12 Irresistible Love, Elaine Anne McAvoy
#13 Eternal Flame, Lurlene McDaniel
#14 Windsong, Linda Herring
#15 Forever Eden, Barbara Bennett
#16 Call of the Dove, Madge Harrah
#17 The Desires of Your Heart, Donna Fletcher Crow
#18 Tender Adversary, Judy Baer
#19 Halfway to Heaven, Nancy Johanson
#20 Hold Fast the Dream, Lurlene McDaniel
#21 The Disguise of Love, Mary LaPietra
#22 Through a Glass Darkly, Sara Mitchell
#23 More Than a Summer's Love, Yvonne Lehman
#24 Language of the Heart, Jeanne Anders

Watch for other books in both the *Serenade Saga* (historical) and *Serenade Serenata* (contemporary) series coming soon.